JUST BE THERE

Author

Gayatri Shankar

RIDHZWORLD
PUBLISHING

Printed & published by:

RidhzWorld Publishing

Hadapsar, Pune, India

www.ridhzworld.com

First Printing Edition, 2023

ISBN 978-81-962000-7-7

PREFACE

'Just Be There' is a compelling story that takes you on a journey of life, love, loss, and acceptance. Losing a loved one is never easy, and the void that they leave behind can be overwhelming. The story will resonate with anyone who has experienced this heartache. The author beautifully captures the process of grieving and how the memories of our loved ones can keep flashing before us, making it difficult to cope with the loss.

However, amidst this dark cloud, the story also highlights the importance of having a good support system. When we are surrounded by people who care for us, the memories of our loved ones don't have to be a source of pain only. We can carry these memories forward and move on with our lives while cherishing their presence in our hearts.

The message of 'Just Be There' is not just limited to dealing with loss. It also brings to light the value of family in a world where everyone is rushing towards success, forgetting who and what is essential. The book features strong characters who may be battling their inner demons, but they understand the importance of togetherness and support.

The story of 'Just Be There' is a reminder that we must be the change we want to see in the world, and it starts with being there for the people who matter to us. The book encourages us to take a moment and reflect on our relationships, reminding us that they are the foundation of our lives and ultimately shape us into who we are.

TABLE OF CONTENTS

CHAPTER 1: THE VOID

All he could hear was, "Abhay!! Abhay!! Please be with me!! I feel like a huge wave of water engulfing me, dragging me away. Please hold my hands. I do not want to go anywhere" and all he could do was shout, "Sandhya….!! Sandhya…!! I am with you. See I am holding you tightly. Nothing will happen, don't worry, I am with you." Then she was gone. "Sandhyaaa!! Sandhya!!" Tears welled up in his eyes which were tightly shut. His body was shaking violently, and he was screaming her name in agony.

"Papa! Are you alright?" A gentle voice was beckoning him. He woke up with a start and looked around. He was completely dazed.

"You dreamt of Mummyji again", spoke his daughter-in-law Anjali gently holding his trembling hands. "I will get you a glass of water. You please relax."

Abhay Singh looked around in his room and his eyes settled on a big photo frame on the wall opposite to his bed. It belonged to his wife, Sandhya. She had passed away a year ago.

Life had come to a standstill for him. The beautiful years which he had spent with her were all just memories now coming back to him on and off.

He had no idea which was real, the one which he had just seen in his dream or the one he was looking at now.

Anjali came back with a glass of water and passed it on to him. He took a sip and looked at her kindly. "Thanks beta, yes, I saw her again. She was in pain…she was scared. I just cannot bear it now. Why did she have to go through this? She was such a beautiful human being. Always cared about others than her own self."

"I know Papa. She has left a big void in our lives. But she is always present with us in our hearts, in our memories."

Abhay got up from his bed slowly. It was already 10am now.

"Papa, you remember about the seminar I told you that you have to attend today. It is at 11.30 am. Ajay is coming to pick you up; get ready now. I have prepared your favourite Aloo Parathas."

Abhay groaned. He had no inclination whatsoever of attending any seminar. Ever since Sandhya had passed away, he had cut off from people and socialising was not exactly on top of his list.

He was now 57 years old but was already feeling like he had turned 75. He had lost around 6kgs of weight, looked pale and tired, his hair had greyed further, and his eyes had sagged with dark circles which were now more prominent. He was a Senior Professor of Computer Science in a top university in Mumbai.

He was no longer going to college although he had received numerous persuasions to join back, from the Dean. He had a huge fan following back in the university, loved by the students and the fellow professors equally. He had left all that behind now.

"Anjali, beta, has Vikram left?" He enquired about his only son Vikram Singh.

Vikram was a bright lad who did all things right when he was a student and scored good marks too. But somewhere down the lane, he was just too weighed down with the expectations of the society and the growing competition and dirty politics that people played these days in order to rise above others.

Not that Vikram was doing bad, he landed himself a good job as a Software Consultant in one of the multinational software companies. But people around him never saw his true potential and he was always dragged into petty politics which he always wanted to steer clear of. He had tried switching jobs a couple of times, but soon realised that they were not doing much to help him. It was the same scenario everywhere. The grass always seemed to be greener on the other side but was not quite actually so.

"Yes Papa, He left quite early today. It seems they have a client visit today and he needs to finish few stuffs urgently. He said he will call you as soon as he gets free." Anjali gave a soft smirk.

Abhay smiled. He knew it was not going to be the case. But he couldn't blame Vikram.

Ever since Sandhya had left, he and Vikram had sort of drifted apart or so it seemed. It was not exactly an obvious one, but both knew it somewhere deep down. It was probably both being unsure of what to say to each other in order to console. They both knew that no words could bring back what they were missing too dearly.

As a result, now Anjali had become a kind of mediator between the two. It was not that both were not talking; they did speak to each other, but it was the mundane stuff. Abhay would ask about Vikram's office and Vikram would enquire about his health and whether he kept his doctor's appointment and so on.

His thoughts were soon interrupted by the doorbell. Abhay started but Anjali waved her hand and said, "You better get ready. I will go check; I think Ajay is home."

Ajay Gupta was 22 but he had the wisdom of a 40-year-old. He was quite mature and understanding for his age unlike the ones who are unsure of what they were doing.

He was a student of Abhay, in fact the brightest one Abhay had ever met as a professor. Abhay had taken an instant liking to the boy who was not only intelligent but also had a very caring nature just like Sandhya. Ajay was like a second son to him.

"Hey Ajay, come on, help yourself with some parathas and lassi." Anjali motioned him to the breakfast table. "Wow sure Bhabhi, I would love to, but we need to hurry, otherwise we will be late for the seminar."

"Papa just got up and will take some time to get ready, Meanwhile, you can finish the parathas". She had a troubled look on her face. Ajay looked at Anjali with a deep concern. "The same dream again? Is he alright?"

Anjali nodded. "He will be fine, that is why you are here, aren't you?" She gave a hopeful smile.

"Yeah, I will try my best to get him back to the same old jolly professor he used to be", said Ajay, unsure of whether this could ever happen.

Ajay gorged on the sumptuous parathas and gulped down the perfectly blended lassi and gave a thumbs up to Anjali. "Heavenly!!". Anjali smiled.

Abhay was dressed up in a light blue formal shirt with thin dark stripes. He wore a dark blue pant which seemed to appear a little loose given that he had lost considerable weight.

"Ajay, how are you doing my boy? It has been a while since we last met." Abhay shook hands with his bright student.

"I am doing good, Sir. Things were a bit too hectic with the mid-term exams. Thank God, they got over 2 days back. So now here I am to meet you", Ajay told while shaking hands with him.

"Papa, please finish the breakfast. Ajay has been patiently waiting for you." Anjali interrupted with a stern look.

"Yes beta. Ajay, please give me 15 mins. Then we are set to go. Let me tell you this and I am sure you are well aware of this, that, I have no interest whatsoever in going out or meeting people. I agreed only because I had promised you that I will tag along."

"I know Sir, but nevertheless I am glad that you are coming. I always enjoy your company."

Abhay gave a weak smile. He knew he could not give good company to people anymore; given the huge disappointment he was, he can only make people further depressed.

He slowly started eating the parathas, his taste buds not quite relishing the flavour. He drank the lassi slowly and thanked Anjali.

"Come Ajay, let us go to wherever you are taking me. Anjali, take care beta, I will be back in the evening and tell Vikram not to worry about me. He has many more important things to worry about right now". Abhay winked at his daughter-in-law.

Abhay then got into Ajay's bike, waved at Anjali, and soon headed for what was going to be the most important event in his life, a life changing one at that!

CHAPTER 2: THE REMINISCENCE

Anjali waved back and settled down on the couch with a cup of hot coffee as Ajay's bike exited from her view. The book that she had been engrossed in, since the last couple of days, was resting on the coffee table with its open pages downwards. It was a beautiful book on how relationships can be nurtured and how trivial matters can sour a healthy relationship.

Three months later, it was going to be her third marriage anniversary with Vikram. She was browsing through the online shopping app to see what the best gift for Vikram would be. Suddenly, the Google Photos App popped up a notification on her smartphone. It was a photo collection which brought up memories from 3 years ago, just three months before her wedding day, the "D Day"!!

She was staring at one particular photo that brought 6 happy, smiling faces alive before her. It was her parents, Abhay, Sandhya, Vikram, and herself who had taken a groupie just at the entrance of 'Second Innings', the old age home for which her parents were primary care givers and contributors.

Rajesh Saini and his wife Sunita Saini were very established dentists who, although in their professional life, brought smiles on people by curing their dental problems, but also believed in bringing smiles on people from within their hearts, especially aged ones.

They had embarked on a journey of supporting a leading old age home called 'Second Innings' which made the second innings memorable for some unfortunate destitute aged members.

Anjali was their only daughter and naturally had been privileged to enjoy all their love and affection. She was a carefree girl who did reasonably well in studies but was more inclined towards arts, especially dance. Dance was something that always brought the best moods out in her.

Soon after finishing her graduation in commerce, she had landed a job in a leading Private Bank as a trainee employee. But five months into it, she was certain that it was not the career for her. She quit her job and started visiting Second Innings and her true calling was soon apparent to her.

It was Second Innings, where she had first met Sandhya 4 years ago and was completely overawed by her charm and presence. Sandhya Singh was a news reader by profession, also wrote blogs on different social issues that plagued the society. Consequently, she did her research by visiting such old age homes and orphanages.

Sandhya had been impressed with the facilities that Second Innings had provided for the elderly. She took time to meet different people, listening to their experiences and Anjali had been the one to take her on the Second Innings-tour-visit. Sandhya was quite charmed by Anjali's honesty and gentle nature and was keen to learn more about her.

Two months after their first encounter, they met each other again. This time it was Second Innings' 10th year Annual function. There was a plethora of events and the old turned into young enthusiastic performers.

Sandhya was a special guest invited along with her family to the event. She had written a superb article on Second Innings which had garnered huge positive response from different people from all walks of life. Subsequently, there were many who came forward with help and funding. Sandhya came along with her husband Abhay and her son Vikram.

The event had been a super success which ended with a solo magnetic dance performance, performed by Anjali that received the maximum applause.

Soon after the event, Sandhya introduced Anjali and her parents to her husband and son. Anjali and Vikram had hit off instantly. Vikram was smitten by Anjali's bubbly and friendly nature. He had already been completely bowled over by her dance performance.

"Your dance performance was exceptionally amazing", Vikram said in a shy tone.

"Thank you so much", Anjali blushed. Anjali was impressed with Vikram's down to earth, shy nature and yet when he spoke, he oozed a certain aura of intelligence and maturity.

Soon it turned into frequent dates for them, and both knew they had developed strong feelings for each other. Both the families got wind of this, and they were ecstatic at this development.

Anjali and Vikram got married a year later in a very unique style. Their wedding was conducted in the Second Innings community hall in a simple manner, yet completely in accordance with their traditions in the presence of their close relatives, friends, and the inmates of Second Innings.

There was no show of wealth on grand parties and exclusive decors and wedding planners.

All that money would be instead used on the development of a trauma care unit within the old age home.

Sandhya and Abhay were an adorable couple. "Anju beta, once you step in as my bahu, I'll leave my job and become your student. I want to learn to play flute from you. It is an absolute delight listening to you", Sandhya had said when she paid an impromptu visit to Second Innings, post Anjali's engagement to Vikram and found her playing 'O Palan hare' to the Second Innings family. Her words still echoed in Anjali's ears.

Anjali's thoughts went back to the last moments which the family had spent with Sandhya before she had left for heavenly abode.

Abhay had been inconsolable, and Vikram was sort of stoned. Both had different ways of dealing with the loss. Abhay was no more the jolly fun-loving professor who was adored by his students. Vikram was no more the sweet and warm natured, he had immersed himself in his work, often became grumpy and impatient with small matters.

Anjali was equally devasted, but she had a huge responsibility to take care of as she had promised her mother-in-law that she would, with all her might and will.

She had to fill the void left by Sandhya and she was determined to do it. The initial 3 months post Sandhya's demise had been too tough for her.

Abhay would frequently pass out and needed to be taken to hospital. Vikram faced career problems compounded with his personal loss, he was on his own warpath. This left Anjali with managing the entire house on her own, taking care of Abhay's doctor visits, medicines and bearing with his emotional upheavals.

During this time, Ajay Gupta, Abhay's most favourite student, had come as a saviour. He was the only person with whom Abhay was comfortable to share his feelings. He had greatly helped Anjali by spending time with Abhay as much as he could by taking time from his busy study schedules.

Vikram was well aware of Ajay's contributions and inwardly grateful to him. What he could not do to help his father, Ajay had done for him.

The sudden whistles of the cooker from the kitchen jolted Anjali from her thoughts back to the present. She fervently prayed for Abhay to bounce back to his normal self.

CHAPTER 3. THE SEMINAR

Ajay made sure to converse frequently with Abhay, while riding the bike so that he doesn't get lost in his thoughts. They reached the venue 10 minutes late than the scheduled time. He parked his bike in the parking lot reserved for special visitors, removed his helmet, and extended his hand to collect Abhay's helmet. "Thank God the traffic was smooth flowing, and the rain Gods were taking a break allowing us to reach as early as possible", he spoke to Abhay while carefully locking his bike and taking out the seminar's entry ticket. Abhay nodded and smiled.

At the entrance, the organisers were arranging few eatery stalls and guiding people towards the seminar hall. "Hi good morning", one of the organisers wished Ajay and Abhay and waited for them to show the entry tickets. Ajay gave a wide smile, wished back the organiser, and showed the tickets. "This way, Sir. Your seats are in the first row. The talk must have begun. So please enter through door 2 as it opens to your row. Have a good day and don't miss the lunch post the seminar." The organisers were polite and knew their job well.

Abhay noticed one of the banners which read – Awaited talk of the Day- How to overcome failure and separation by Shivani Gupta, a PG diploma in Yoga and a student counsellor.

Abhay's steps slowed down to read the banner. Ajay too changed his pace and looked at what he was focusing on; he was relieved to find him reading the banner and inwardly in his mind ticked the second check point. The first was to make sure he accompanied him to the seminar and the second was to see to it that he gets to learn the topic and the speaker on his own.

As they neared the door, Abhay was in two minds; he wished to turn around and get back home as he did not want to meet his students and colleagues but a part of him desired to listen to the talk and a part of him knew Ajay must have realised his thoughts; And, yes, Ajay had realised his favourite professor's dilemma. "Sir, let us go in. I'll make sure to stay next to you each second during and after the seminar till I drop you back home. We can exit through the special guests' door as I have the green pass. We have a special lunchroom where only the speakers, the Dean, the Director, and few organisers will be present." Ajay explained like a parent bribing their 2-year-old kid to get inside a doctor's cabin for a routine check-up.

Abhay knew Ajay will come out with all possible solutions for any problem, just like Sandhya. He smiled at him and decided to step in but before that he popped the question which Ajay was waiting for. "How and why have we got green passes?"

"Because Shivani Gupta is my aunt, and you are my favourite professor." Ajay replied with a twinkle in his eyes and opened door 2 for Abhay to enter. Now, a larger part of him wanted to hear the talk.

"Failure is when you do not try. When you try and realise it is not working the way you want it, then it is not failure, it doesn't mean you are inferior or dumb. It simply means that you have learnt more, and you have a reason to start afresh. In the first step, never compete with others, compete with yourself which is the primary move towards success."

There was a round of applause from a few students. One of the students spoke over the mike attached at her desk. "Good morning, ma'am. Taking the privilege to interrupt you because you asked us to consider you as our friend. I wish our parents get to hear you."

Shivani smiled and said, "After all the failures, there will be a time when we succeed. You can explain your parents after that and make sure at least the next generation doesn't participate in the rat-race of proving things to others. Prove your worth to yourself."

Her presentation, her simplicity, her choice of words bowled everyone present there. Abhay, after a long time, was more attentive to someone's talk without entering his world.

"Once the umbilical cord is cut, the baby is separated from the mother's womb and enters a new world. The babies learn to survive with only crying and smiling as their medium of language. Don't you think the Almighty taught us the toughest lesson of how to tackle separation within few moments of our birth?"

Abhay suddenly felt a wave of emotions hitting him. Ajay sensed his restlessness and handed him a bottle of water. He excused himself for a break. Ajay accompanied him to the open garden and breathed fresh air. The word separation made him remember Sandhya. Ajay waited patiently for 5 minutes and then spoke, "Sir, shall we go in? when a small baby is able to tackle a big problem, don't you think even we can?"

Abhay was wonderstruck at Ajay's maturity. He, in his mind, appreciated Ajay's parents for his upbringing and followed him back to the auditorium.

"You may face the pain of physical separation from your parents, friends, lover, wife/ husband, siblings, kids, or colleagues. Brooding over it day in and out and forcibly getting isolated from the rest of the world will never alleviate the suffering. To bluntly put, it is your mode of escapism from the stark reality. Eventually this sorry state would be going to affect not just you but result in mental agony for all the others who love you, souring the relationship and congenial rapport after a certain point of time".

"There was this lady who lost her lover and fiancé just a few days before her marriage in a car accident. She was in a terrible trauma for almost one year. She had built a wall around herself and cut off from her dear ones. This caused a lot of mental agony to everyone around her. Do you know who this lady was?" Her short pause after this statement led to another shocking revelation. "The lady is none other than me", she calmly let out, causing many gasps, and left many with widened eyes and increased attention. Abhay sat abrupt in his seat, feeling a strong connection.

She smiled and continued, "It has been 25 years now since he passed away. Do you think that I do not feel for him or remember him? There has not been a single day when I don't think of him. But you see there is a difference here. He is my biggest strength now and always inspires me to face any kind of problem in life. I miss him but do not spend that time in agony, rather I convert our memories into happy thoughts and try to share the same with others. With the help of my well-wishers and my Yoga Guru, I have now come a long way and reached this position.

I want you all to spread your wings, explore and spill happiness wherever you are; utilise every moment of your life, accept and overcome the challenges thrown at you with grace. How do you do it? Pursue some form of art or develop hobbies or meet a lot of people or meditate, whichever makes you happy and doesn't harm the others around you. I'll be teaching a few yoga forms and meditation in the next session to keep your mind at peace which will support you to accept the reality of life." Saying so, she tapped a few keys on her laptop and projected a page on the white board using the over-head projector, which read:

Chalti Chakki Dekh Kar, Diya Kabira Roye
Dui Patan Ke Beech Mein, Sabit Bacha Na Koye

She explained, "Looking at the grinding stones, Kabir laments - In the duel of wheels, nothing stays intact. *Dui Patan* here signifies earth (*Prithvi*) and sky (*Akash*) and within the ambit of these is all creation and life as also the manifestation of all-natural phenomenon of dualities: day and night, life and death, joys, and sorrows, thereby making life forever in motion (*Chalti Chakki*) and an ever-changing process. Trapped in this duality, whatever we see is perishable. Nothing that we comprehend is eternal."

She ended the session with a Kabir's Doha which beautifully summarised her topic. She was given a standing ovation and all the 184 pairs of eyes displayed the enthusiasm to attend the next session.

Abhay looked at Ajay and held his hand tightly to support himself and thanked him for being with him. Ajay ticked the third and the last point. The change had begun.

CHAPTER 4: THE BRAIN-STORMED

He stood at the railway platform desperately waiting for the train to arrive; his look was that of a marooned sailor. A few minutes ago, he had sprinted towards the platform with the final burst of energy that was left in him just to see the train leaving. Vikram could barely breathe but still managed to hurl a string of curses about the train timing that drew a few amusing glances.

"Whatever happened to these Mumbai local trains", he wondered! "How could they be so punctual when not needed!! A mere thirty second delay would have ensured his boarding. It was already 10 pm. Another 15 min of wait before the next train arrived", he groaned. He did not like that time was getting wasted like this. That too when he was going home.

He wore a light green coloured checked formal shirt and a black pant. Whatever average lustre his attire seemed to have had in the morning had completely lost its trace. His shirt was soaked with sweat and was almost out of the tuck in; The pant which had earlier tightly clung to his paunches had now started giving in to the gravitational pull. His black shoes were now dust brown. His office identity card was swaying left to right. His 'boulder' bag was pressing on to his shoulder nerves. Or was it getting onto his nerves!!

"I am quite a sight", he thought. But he did not care. He used to, once, but not anymore. He sometimes wondered whether he had undergone a life transformation. Well, yes, he had, in some ways, but then who does not?

He wiped his face first and then the face of his Smartphone. There were a few missed calls from his wife, Anjali. His fingers involuntarily launched the WhatsApp and started typing the template. His messages were becoming more and more templates driven recently." Missed train. Will be late. Call you later. No charge". That was fairly easy. Thank you, technology!! Conversation was not the need of the hour. Something else was.

He could feel his stomach rumbling and cramps kicking in. It had been a good 8 hours since lunch. He had missed his evening junk snacks today. Not that he loved having them, but then they pacified him, at least for a while.

But then nothing that happened today in office was routine; nothing that could really pacify him. He clenched his fists at those thoughts, but soon calmed himself. This is not the time. Prioritize!! Perhaps, the only good thing that he could see about today was that it was a Friday. He had two full days to get over whatever happened.

A distant spot of light somehow seemed to bring a ray of hope to him. The train arrived; He was pushed, and he shoved as well; Here take it! He found a comfortable corner for him to stand just below the fan. Ahh!! He was becoming a connoisseur at this. Let the others shove to find seats; he was not keen on finding a seat. His job had made sure that he despised sitting, even if he was dead tired. His mind went back to the events that had transpired earlier today, culminating into a huge volcano that was waiting to erupt inside his head. He quickly closed his eyes for a few seconds and then opened them.

The man standing next to him was watching a South Indian movie dubbed in Hindi where the hero was using a football to knock out a group of thugs like a game of bowling pins. To add to their woes, he even spun the ball like the way Lord Krishna would use His Sudarshan Chakra!!A quick smirk curled around his lips as he pictured this particular scene with the people who had ruined his day in office. How he wished he knocked them down like that! It would not suffice though. He was jolted back to reality by the crunching halt at the next station. Another surge of crowd started shoving him. Get off guys!

Things settled soon and he directed his gaze to the other side at a couple sweet talking to each other. The girl was leaning onto the partition board while the guy surrounded her putting his arms around her protectively and giving dagger looks to the other men staring at them. They appeared to be excitedly talking about a new movie released, the guy trying his luck teasing his girlfriend, while she was constantly pretending to get irritated and showing her punching and pinching abilities to her boyfriend. He sighed and made a disgruntled face. "Why all this PDA!!", his reaction was quite subtle but did not go unnoticed; the other commuters seeing this gave a knowing smile.

Two more stations to go, he thought. His stomach cramps stopped by themselves realizing the futility of tempting him for food. The next supreme thing had taken priority now. Sleep! It was dangerous to doze off now as he could miss getting down. That was the last thing he wanted, considering how 'well' his day had gone today. He kept his eyes wide open though they tried their best not to budge. He gulped the last sip from his apparently empty water bottle.

Finally!! The train arrived at the station, and he braced himself. He quickly sprinted down the platform stairs and towards the auto stand which was always messed up with the drivers and the passengers' negotiating fares.

People, at his hour, had energy to argue and look for a share commute!! But he had neither time nor energy for that. 'Rickshaw, Street 10', he yelled at the auto driver standing first in the queue. The driver thanked his luck inwardly with a mock gaze at the other fuming jealous drivers. 'Seventy rupees as it is past 11pm now', he smiled triumphantly at his prized passenger who did not even bother to reply but just nodded as he got in and closed his eyes. He sucked in the cool night breeze as much as he could, while waiting to reach home as early as possible. Finally, he entered the lift of his building and pressed the 3rd floor button. He so wanted to hit the pillow and doze off but somehow felt the need to fill up his rumbling stomach first.

Anjali opened the door and hugged him, and he returned the same albeit weakly. He sat under the shower; he desperately needed that. In a way, he wanted to get rid of the grime surrounding him, not just on his body but also in his thoughts. He let the shower water run all over his body, squeezed about a quarter of the shampoo bottle on his head. A whole bar of soap was almost reduced to half its size. He did not get up from his trance until his wife started knocking at the bathroom door.

Another twenty minutes went in silence as he dressed and quickly finished his dinner without starting any conversation with Anjali. She knew this and did the same as she had learnt and sort of mastered this art. Read his mood!!

As soon as he hit the bed, he started fiddling with his phone. He launched the Facebook App and started scrolling through the news feeds involuntarily. He closed Facebook and opened WhatsApp; 120 messages from a school group he had muted. He had a strong feeling to exit the group, but exiting will have raised more questions so he just left it as it without reading a single message.

Anjali switched off the lights, slowly crept into the bed and put an arm over him lovingly. He thought he probably had nyctophobia or had perhaps started behaving like one recently. He closed his eyes praying silently!! In the midst of all this, he had completely forgotten to ask her about his father.

In another room, just a few feet away, Abhay was lying down on his bed and his mind went back to the events that had transpired earlier that day, on the seminar given by Shivani Gupta!!

CHAPTER 5. THE DAWN

The incessant downpour of rains continued to batter the Mumbai city. The street where Abhay's family lived was completely inundated and the stray dogs were barking on top of their voices as they were dualling with each other to secure themselves a safe shelter. The streetlights flickered barely with whatever grace they could show before they went off.

It was apparent that the clouds were enjoying a Friday late night dance party as they thundered with all their might. The resultant wave of lightning sparkled up the entire street on and off.

Abhay was watching all these from his bedroom windows, albeit absent-mindedly, as he lay down sideward on his bed in an awkward position as the pillow was further pressing down his spondylitis nerves. He shifted uncomfortably on his bed as his thoughts went back to the words that clearly echoed in his ears. The voice of Shivani Gupta was causing him a sense of discomfort.

"Brooding over your sorrow day in and out and forcibly getting isolated from the rest of the world will never alleviate the suffering. Honestly, it is your mode of escapism from the stark reality. Eventually this sorry state will not only affect just you but result in mental agony for all the others surrounding you, those who love you, those who want you to be happy. Please understand this. The mind is everything; What you think you become."

Something in those harsh yet honest words had pricked Abhay where it hurt him the most. He looked at the ever-smiling Sandhya peacefully staring at him through the wooden frame.

"Abhay what have you done to yourself?", he heard Sandhya talking to him, her voice choked with emotions.

"Look at you! The Abhay I fell in love with was not like this. He was always cheerful, always brought smile on everyone; You are a different person whom I don't know."

Abhay's eyes welled with tears as he pictured himself in the last one year.

He had quit his job; stopped calling his friends, he barely went out of his house. He had developed sleep disorders and was taking pills. His doctor had frequently advised him to try out different things like pursuing hobbies, his passion, talk to friends, but he had ignored all these advice as he felt nobody could really understand him as they were not going through the trauma he was facing.

However, the way Shivani had put across her thoughts had made Abhay realise how guilty he had been, of causing hardships to others in his family. Vikram and Anjali were dealing with it too and instead of supporting them, he had been adding to their woes.

Anjali had to put up with two broken men who were so engrossed in their own miseries. When she had arrived in the family, Sandhya and Abhay had promised her parents that they would take care of her as their own daughter and keep her always happy. Anjali took utmost care of him when he was sick and was always there to support him. He had done nothing to reciprocate.

"And Vikram! My dear child, you needed your father to take care of you, guide you in this journey of life. You wanted me to be there as a pillar of strength. But I built my own walls and did not even let you through", Abhay was feeling overwhelmed with each and every growing thought. He saw himself in the mirror with his face drenched with sweat even in the chilly rainy atmosphere. More than the clouds thundering outside, Abhay was feeling disoriented by these guilt thoughts roaring inside his mind.

He held his pillow tightly and shut his eyes trying to calm himself down. A sudden flurry of words gave him hope. It is never too late to mend. Reach out and seek help. People are there to support you. I am there to help. All that you need is your own will.' Shivani's words now were soothing him. He did not realise when he dozed off.

It was a beautiful Saturday morning with not a trace of the dark clouds hovering above the tall buildings. Abhay had woken up early even though he had not slept well the previous night. He used to do this with Sandhya every morning while enjoying a cup of hot tea. Abhay recalled the way she admired Mother Nature and made him cultivate the habit too.

Once Vikram entered the secondary schooling, their mornings would begin at 5:30am and Abhay would go for a morning walk. He used to get back by 6:30am and then drop Vikram at school. Sandhya, by then, used to get their masala tea ready and wait for Abhay to get back from school; post which they settled in their balcony with their tea and enjoyed watching the sky, clouds, trees, birds, the morning joggers, the school going children and the office goers.

Today, he missed Sandhya but made sure not to become weak. “Some things are better taught and explained by a teacher. The people around you may spend eons making you learn or realize a point but only a teacher will be able to rightly hammer the lesson in the student’s mind. A few raw and blunt sentences from a teacher, while teaching, make the students realise their fault soon. Don’t ever feel bad if you are exposed to such sentences by your teachers, think over it and take the next step towards success. Sometimes sweet talks may not give the required result but a blunt talk where the person is exposed to the reality will only pump-up sense in the brain.” Abhay remembered his teacher’s farewell talk and was able to relate to his present circumstances. Only when Shivani stated that this was a mode of escapism and souring other relations did he realise the truth.

Anjali who was setting the breakfast kept checking on Abhay from the kitchen. Vikram reached the breakfast table and took out the newspaper for a quick glance. The layoffs going on in the IT sector was one of the major headlines. He shook his head and put down the paper.

His eyes fell on the plants in their balcony and on his father, who was standing near those plants looking at the playground below. Just then he realised that he had forgotten to enquire about the seminar. “Good morning, Papa. How was the seminar?” Vikram’s question broke the morning silence and Abhay’s trance.

“Good morning, Vikram and Anjali beta”, he replied with a smile.

There was something different in his eyes which Anjali was quick to notice. She sensed a renewed vigour in his demeanour. She knew it had something to do with yesterday’s seminar.

“Yes, the seminar was interesting. I did gain a new perspective. I want to know more about this Shivani Gupta. I never knew Ajay’s aunt was a yoga trainer and motivational speaker.”

“That is nice Papa, finally you found something interesting”, Vikram was relieved.

Anjali still had no clue why Vikram had been so frustrated the day before and planned to ask him once things settled down.

“Vikram, I was thinking if we all can visit Siddhivinayak temple today evening.” Another surprise for Anjali. Before Vikram could open his mouth to say anything, Anjali intervened.

“Sure Papa, why not!! It has been ages since we last visited Siddhivinayak temple”.

She wanted to start things afresh with the blessings of Lord Ganesh. Vikram nodded, but he was not too excited about it.

Abhay knew that it was high time that he brought around positive changes not only in him but also more importantly, it was needed in Vikram and Anjali’s lives. Their life had just started, and it was very important to bring it on track. Why did he not realise it before? He had been selfish enough for a long time, he rued.

One thing that Abhay had resolved now was that no matter how weak he was, how low he felt, he was not going to make Vikram or Anjali suffer anymore. And only one person can help me in this, perhaps. Shivani Gupta! He planned to make a call to Ajay soon. “But let me first apologise to Ganpati Bappa and seek his blessing”, Abhay thought to himself.

CHAPTER 6: THE MENDED

They had met on the first day of their post-graduation program. They hit it off instantly. Every single day they met each other in the library for 10 minutes. Their eyes spoke a lot; they wished to talk to each other and spend time alone but due to the fear of the teachers, society, and parents, continued with their 10 minutes-library-love story. He was a no-nonsense young man who seldom beat around the bush; she got to know this when he secretly slipped a note in her hand which read, "Let us finish our exams and I'll visit your parents with my family and then get married".

As promised, he visited her home with his parents' right after their final exams and confessed his love for her to her parents. She was scared of her father's and brother's reaction. "Rohit spoke to me about Shivani on the day he spotted her in college", his mom laughed. Shivani was standing with her mom in the kitchen avoiding her mother's dagger looks at her. Amrita who had entered Shivani's family few months before as her brother's wife, was unsure of what to say but held Shivani's arm and with her eyes and smile assured her that all will go well.

His dad filled in with a few more convincing statements and finally her family agreed. The betrothal was fixed in the upcoming month and their wedding was fixed early next year which meant they had 8 months to plan and shop for their wedding. In the meanwhile, he got a bank job, and she became a teacher. He had applied for leave a couple of weeks before their wedding as they had decided to conduct the wedding at his native place in Punjab. It was the last day at his office as a bachelor; his family along with Shivani's family were to catch the train from CST at 9:00pm. He had left from his office at 6:00pm and taken a taxi; it was 8.30pm and he hadn't reached the station. The panic in everyone's eyes was evident; She was scared, nervous and vulnerable. One of his office colleagues and his good friend who knew where his family members will be, came running to the station. He spoke to his elder brother and father, and they looked at his mom, then Shivani and her family. Shivani felt the bile rise up her in her gut and sat down; she knew she heard his friend say 'accident...hospital...'.

Amrita and Rakesh sprang on to their feet to support Shivani; they all proceeded to the hospital where they got to know that Rohit had lost his life immediately after the accident; it was a truck which had broken the signal and rammed into his taxi. Shivani's world collapsed; she was broken inside-out; she remembered all those sweet moments with him, his smile, his simple way of living, those 15 letters in the span of two and half years of knowing each other, their first photo with each other which they had got snapped after their engagement near the gateway of India using his camera, and all of a sudden she let out a huge cry as the feeling of having lost him started sinking in her heart.

It took her 2 years to completely come out of the cocoon which she had built around herself. She learnt a lot during these two years and pledged to help people in trauma.

She utilised the evening time to learn yoga and in due course did all the needed certifications to become a professional yoga instructor. As a teacher, she came across students facing a lot of issues with their studies or with the pressure of improving grades or with their personal lives which hampered their day-to-day routines. She pursued a bachelors in psychology and slowly moved on to become a student counsellor. She kept herself fully occupied with her studies and her eagerness to learn new things. She started conducting counselling programs in many parts of the country and along with this made sure to guide her students to maintain calmness during a storm. Her learnings in Yoga and psychology helped her in dealing with her students in a diverse way and gained a lot of popularity. She made sure to visit her brother and family once in a month and stay for a couple of days.

Today, 25 years later, she sat on the bamboo swing in the balcony, sipping a glass of lemonade to beat the heat, she felt the note, which she had got laminated and smiled at her first love letter. She had never married and had dedicated her life to support people and help them come out of their sufferings.

"Shivani tai kaam zala…me zaau aata? (My work is done …shall I leave now)", the maid stood at the balcony door and asked her. Shivani smiled and added, "Thank you Durga! Udya bhetu (see you tomorrow)". Durga smiled on hearing her speak Marathi.

Durga had been working at her brother's place for the last 25 years. She was more of a family member than a maid. She was few years younger to Shivani; Durga too had played a great role in Shivani's recovery. When Amrita and Rakesh were off to their respective jobs, Durga had made sure to give Shivani a good company and kept her mind occupied by asking her to teach her basic mathematics and English or by playing antakshari. During those time Shivani was not confident to speak in Marathi though she understood and managed to make small conversations; she had asked Durga to converse with her in Marathi in order to gain a grip over the language.

"If she had received a formal education, she would have become a great psychologist", Shivani told Amrita when they were talking about Durga. "She reads my mind even before I understand what it says and does something to prevent me from zoning out", Shivani was all praise about Durga.

Shivani closed the main door after seeing Durga climbing down the stairways and went inside to check on her brother Rakesh who had returned from his offshore duties in the wee hours of the morning. He was fast asleep. Shivani flashed a loving smile looking at her brother sleep like a kid. He had been a pillar to her when she was in trouble; he had persuaded her to move on and get married but later when he realized that she is happy staying single; he had supported her decision whole heartedly. Amrita, Rakesh's wife, had stood by Shivani through thick and thin and helped her with her in setting up her Yoga centre once she became a professional.

'Bua, if you wish to learn Analysis of Algorithm and design then I bet you may seldom find a professor like Abhay Sir. Wow! He is superb!' Ajay spoke to Shivani during one of her visits to his place. From then on, every semester Ajay used to have one subject taught by Prof Abhay Singh, so she used to hear him talk about Abhay sir and appreciate his teaching style every time they met.

She had eventually heard about Sandhya's demise and Abhay's descent into an abyss. But she had been out of India for almost a year for a special course.

Now that she was back to India and was somewhat aware of Abhay's current situation, she planned to do something about it. The seminar had been the first step.

CHAPTER 7. THE PLUNGE

Abhay was seated on a plush bear sized black sofa across the reception desk. The sweet aroma of the mandarin oil rising from the perfume diffuser filled his nostrils and he took another whiff to calm down his mind which was currently juggling with a thousand random thoughts. The AC did little to cool his sweating face. He kept looking at his watch and then at the reception desk. He looked around and was impressed with the entire getup that the Yoga studio had to offer. "Just Be There", as it was called, was located in a prime locality where it could be easily accessed.

Abhay had booked an appointment with Shivani at 11.30 am. It was already time, and he was getting more and more restless with each passing second. Ajay had offered to accompany him, but he had declined saying that it was his own fight with his demons; But now he regretted that decision. What was he actually going to talk about?

Finally, his patience was answered as the receptionist motioned to him and said that Shivani has summoned him. She led him towards a series of rooms that seemed to be Yoga, Music, and Dance rooms; he entered the main meeting room where Shivani was seated behind a table.

She wore a bright green embroidered saree; her green-rimmed spectacles complemented her attire perfectly, accentuating her looks. Abhay now noticed that behind those slightly wrinkled features and thick rimmed specs was a pretty face which was quite charming and at the same time depicted a lot of maturity. She smiled at him and shook hands with him gently.

"Professor Abhay, nice to meet you." Her voice was gentle and kind. "Ajay has spoken a great deal about you that I am also quite a fan of you now. In fact, every time we talk, he had something or the other to say about your exceptional teaching abilities." Abhay could sense the honesty in her voice, and he knew that she was not the kind who would just indulge in vain flattery.

"I…err...Ma'am, I don't know what he has said about me, but he really regards me high, I am not even sure if I am that worthy", Abhay said sheepishly.

"No professor, you must not think that way. Once in a while, accepting an adulation someone has for you does not hurt, does it?" She laughed. "And please, you can call me Shivani. One of the principal rules in our Yoga Studio is that only. We address each other by their first name regardless of age. That gives us a sense of oneness with each other and helps me to connect better with my clients and vice-versa".

"Sure, Ma'am…sorry I mean Shivani, you can call me Abhay too."

"Well Abhay, I do know to some extent on what you have been through, and Ajay told me that you have stopped visiting college too." Abhay was surprised. He had no idea of what and how much did Shivani know about him. However, it did break the ice and he felt more comfortable now while talking to Shivani.

“I do not know what to say, but ever since Sandhya left me, I have kind of lost every interest. Or…I guess I should say that I had lost interest in everything, but your speech made me realise the trouble I was giving others who love me. Thank you, ma’am…err…. Shivani. I was in a profession in which we were required to address our colleagues, seniors, or juniors, as Madam or Sir; Old Habits die hard”, saying so he smiled looking at Shivani.

She returned his smile, nodded understandingly, and added “I feel pleased to hear my speech brought a change, Abhay. Should I tell Ajay that he can expect his favourite professor in his final semester?”, she ventured.

He looked down at his feet. ‘I really don’t know. the thought of facing my colleagues and my students freaks me out I am unable to focus on one particular thing. I just get lost into my own thoughts and zone out…I think…I don’t know…I just can’t live like this. I don’t want to live without Sandhya “he started crying softly and his voice was choked, he was lost for words when she stood from her chair, filled a glass of water and offering it to him spoke, ’Abhay, don’t worry and don’t push yourself too hard; take one step at a time and slowly you will find the Abhay whom Sandhya loves.’ He nodded his head hearing this and smiled at her choice of words.

‘Sandhya loves…that was nice to hear. I wish you both had met when she was alive.”

“Yes, I really missed meeting such a wonderful soul” Shivani replied.
“Here, listen, why don’t you share something about her. How you met each other? What do you like about her the most?” She wanted him to keep in the conversation as she knew that the more, he would come forward with his feelings, the faster he would be able to come out of his trauma.

“We met for the very first time when she had accompanied the news-channel crew for conducting a quiz event in my college; I had just joined my college as an Assistant professor, and she was doing her internship with the News Channel. I was designated to coordinate with the crew on behalf of our college and she was appointed as the spokesperson to coordinate with the college authorities to design the schedule. This led to our frequent meetings. Those 15 days of knowing each other and working as a team made us realise that we should team-up with each other forever”. Abhay wiped his eyes with his handkerchief. Shivani was listening to him intently.

“You see, I was smitten by her bubbly nature, I was somewhat the opposite, I was jolly too but nothing in front of her. I take time to gel with people, the initial starting trouble has always been there. But Sandhya was completely crazy. The happy go lucky, enjoy life to the fullest kind. She believed in seeing people happy around her. She was never into competing with anyone or surpassing anyone. She said each individual is good at something or the other. If I am better than someone in a particular field, then that person may be much better than me in something else. So, one must never belittle anyone in life.

Always encourage the person around you to do better and you will see that you will automatically do better too. This is the quality that I loved about her. She was never arrogant about anything she possessed nor was she jealous of something she did not. The add-on was she was too good in her work; She was the perfectionist in whatever work she did."

Shivani was impressed with Abhay's undeniable love for his wife. She felt a wave of sympathy for him to have lost Sandhya too early.

"I can fully understand the position Sandhya holds in your life. Now let me make it simple for you. You have a son and a daughter-in-law who love you and want you to be happy; what would Sandhya have wanted from you in this situation? I am sure that she always wanted you to be happy in life, keep your family happy, guide your children to do the right thing. Are you doing what Sandhya wants you to do?"

Abhay was in great anguish. He knew what Shivani said made full sense. He was a wreckage himself, but his family was suffering because of him. Vikram was not living the life that he and Sandhya had wished for him.

"That is why I have come here Shivani. I do not want my family to suffer anymore. You are my only hope."

"Do you know why this studio is called 'Just Be There', Abhay?" This is the inspiration I got from Rohit, my fiancé; Whenever I used to feel very low, I would just look up at the sky and say Just Be There Rohit and trust me he would be there."

"You need to do the same Abhay, and Sandhya will be there always to guide you. And don't worry I am there too."

Abhay started to leave as his appointment was over now. He was going to be here again soon as Shivani had given him a course schedule for 5 sessions with her, one session every Wednesday and Saturday.

CHAPTER 8: THE ARTIST

"Good morning, Abhay", Shivani greeted when Abhay entered for the next session. Abhay smiled and wished her back. She gestured him to sit on the chair and took out 2 cups to serve tea. "Green or Black?", she questioned. "I don't prefer these. Sorry. I prefer tea with milk", Abhay told her. She placed back one of the two cups inside and took out a glass, filled it with water and handing it over to him asked, "Do you know which day is today?".

Abhay had a confused look on his face and nodded his head while inside his head he was trying to find out what was it that he has missed. She smiled at his confused look and sipping tea spoke, "Abhay, 2 years back did you not celebrate 30 years of your teaching life? Ajay had sent me those photos in the morning; That was the year you had started teaching him; he even shared a video". Saying so she unlocked her phone and showed him the video. Abhay was playing the tabla for the vocalist who was singing the Abhang- '*omkara pradhana roop ganeshache*'.

"Have you got some formal training in playing tabla?", she questioned. He smiled as he remembered his childhood days and spoke, "My father was working for the railways; He was a station master. Every day I used to go to the railway station to deliver his lunch before going to school. He used to enjoy eating home made fresh food; my mom used to make me carry a 4-tier lunch box consisting of a round meal. It was one such day when I had gone to deliver the lunch box when I saw my father talking to a man of his age. As I approached them, my father beckoned me to fasten my pace and meet his friend. "Abhay beta, this is my classmate, Arvind Mulwankar, the famous Tabla artist. Come take his blessings. I quickly followed what my dad told and touched his feet to take blessings."

"Arvind, it will be great to see my son get a formal training in tabla. I have noticed him drum the vessels and the table and produce some good beats." Abhay paused for a second, looked at Shivani who was curious to know the rest of the story.

"Arre waah beta! Yes, I'll surely teach if you are genuinely interested" Arvind ji looked at me and I nodded my head with the widest smile. It was an unforgettable moment to meet an artist whom I admired and was a fan of his concerts; that's how I ended up learning Tabla under his guidance. Abhay was nostalgic and added, "Ah! Those beautiful days…seems like yesterday."

Shivani patiently heard him throwing the right expressions at the right junctures. She had hit the correct note and the session began with Abhay getting involved completely. Though she never expected him to come out with so many details for answering her question, she was happy to listen to him.

Abhay on the other hand realised that he had spoken this much and that too with full involvement after a long time. He was happy to see someone sitting next to him and patiently hearing him out. He remembered the school days when he used to return back home and share every single detail with his mother; his mother made sure to listen to every word he spoke with complete attention.

"So, you are an amazing professor, a great tabla player, a good and obedient son, a loving family man. Wow! Abhay...interesting to know you". Shivani's words were like nectar to his ears. He felt the same happiness which a child feels when he is appreciated by his/her parents.

"Where is the tabla now?", she asked. "Anjali must have kept it safe. After dinner, Anjali used to play the flute and I used play the tabla and Sandhya and Vikram were good audience, who sometimes used to hum the tunes that we played", Abhay replied.

"Don't you think you should start this practice again? You can count me and Ajay as your audience during weekends", Shivani sounded happy and was curious to know his answer.

He nodded his head but didn't voice out the answer as he was unsure of himself; he was not sure whether he will take out the tabla after getting back home; even if he takes it out, cleans it and tunes it, he knew he may become emotional playing it as he will remember his parents and Sandhya and the way they enjoyed the music he produced.

"Abhay it is fine if you don't want me and Ajay to visit your home but don't forget to record it and send. We will enjoy listening to it sitting at home", seeing his reaction Shivani was quick to add this and successfully bring him out of the trance as Abhay smiled and said, "it will bring back lot of old memories and…", she cut him mid-way and said, "then that's nice to remember and cherish those memories, right?'

Abhay did not say anything; He was just unsure of what to say to Shivani. "Let us do one thing Abhay, you must have known by now that we have got some special attention to arts, we do arrange for music and dance sessions in addition to the usual yoga and meditation courses. We have got one ice-breaking session for your batch-mates after two days and what I want you to do is come prepared with a tabla note for any one of your favourite songs or bhajans. You will be performing for 15 to 20 mins. Take this as your first assignment here.

"A concert by the great Tabla artist Abhay Singh", she laughed. Abhay looked trapped. But, at the same time, he knew this was a great way to face his fears and gain confidence. It had been a while since he had played the tabla, so now was the time to clear off the dust and start again.

That evening Abhay was ransacking his room when Anjali entered. "Papa what have you been doing", she asked, exasperated, as she coughed seeing all the dust that was now filling her nostrils. "Tell me what you want, and I will look for it."

Abhay looked down at her from the stool he was standing at. He had been searching for the loft from one corner to the other and removing dirty cans, old suitcases, buckets everything he could see in the loft. "Where is the tabla?", he asked continuing his search.

"It is not in this room Papa; I have kept it in the master-bedroom's loft along with my music notes. I will get it for you", saying so Anjali left the room.

Abhay felt pissed at himself for not asking before and spending almost half an hour in vain. Anjali was pleasantly surprised as she knew that Shivani had awakened his passion for the Tabla again. She quickly retrieved the Tabla and slightly dusted them off and brought them to the hall.

Abhay carefully placed them on a smooth clean fabric and started to tap them slowly, his ears carefully listening to the beats.

"Let us play Paayoji Meine Ram Rattan Dhan Paayo song", Anjali announced and raced off to get her flute.

Abhay closed his eyes and started to hum the song inwardly trying to remember the beats and made a mental simulation of the entire note he was about to play tabla for.

Anjali quickly sent a WhatsApp message to Ajay, "Your Aunt is brilliant, Ajay. She made Papa look out for his Tabla. He is preparing himself to play Tabla now. Please thank her on my behalf."

Ajay was overjoyed to hear this. "Excellent Bhabhi…we will get Abhay Sir back to his old self." He knew what he had planned today morning had worked perfectly.

CHAPTER 9: THE ASK

"Hello Mummy, how was your trip to Amritsar?", Anjali was sitting in her balcony on the small cushion chair and talking to her mom, Sunita. Anjali's parents had gone on a trip to Amritsar for a week and had just returned and reached home. They stayed in the street next to the one where Abhay stayed, and it was just a 10 min walk to their house.

"It was almost very well except that your dad got one of his legs slightly sprained while boarding the train. But he is better now. I massaged his legs with Iodex", Sunita replied.

"Oh no! Shall I come now? Is it too bad?", Anjali asked with concern.

"Don't worry Anju, he is just lying on the bed. I will be preparing something for lunch and then will sleep for a while. We are just tired after the journey".

"How many times I have told you Mummy, don't take the train journey, travel by flight, but you never listen to me", Anjali was annoyed.

"Arey, you don't know the fun we have in train, and we are not in any hurry so why take the flight and sit glued to the seat feeling so restricted. Do you know how much we relished the Chole Kulche at Amritsar station!! We did not miss the lassi too, it was heavenly."

Anjali smiled. These little happy moments that you enjoy during travel are really worthwhile than some of the bigger luxuries.

"I am going to pack lunch for you both and get them. You must be dead tired", Anjali offered, looking at the clock. It was 11am now. She should be done with the lunch preparation and then visit her parents by 12.30 pm.

Sunita started to protest but then decided to let Anjali do as she wished. They were anyway eager to meet their daughter and give her the gifts that they had got for Anjali, Vikram, and Abhay.

"Sure Ma, I will go prepare now. See you soon." Anjali cut the call and kept her mobile for charging.

"Radhika Didi, have you soaked the Rajma; what about Aloo? Please peel them and also cut Cauliflower and tomato. I am going to keep basmati rice in the cooker now. The menu for today is Rajma Chawal, Mixed vegetable sabzi and Rotis. I have to pack them for mummy daddy too."

"Yes, Anjali ji, I have them all ready, I will quickly chop cauliflower and tomatoes. How was their trip?", enquired Radhika who was five years elder to Anjali; although her primary role was sweeping, mopping, and cleaning the utensils, she also helped Anjali in cooking by keeping all ingredients ready, chopping, peeling, and sometimes making Rotis.

"Yes Didi, they had a wonderful trip, they have got some new frocks and salwar kameez for Pihu", Anjali replied.

Pihu was Radhika's 7-year-old daughter. She was a sweet intelligent girl whom Anjali's parents adored.

"Arre Anjali ji, they just got her 2 dresses recently on her birthday." Radhika was feeling awkward. She knew that Anjali was very sweet and would always help her out in tough situations. Radhika's husband was a happy go lucky person who would not stick to one job. He had already changed 5 jobs that year. Although he was computer literate and knew basic skills like maintaining excels, data entry and stuff, he would get bored easily and quit his job in as less as 3 months durations.

This, often, put Radhika in tight spots as they had to bear the rent expenses, Pihu's school fees and also her mother-in-law's medical expenses.

Radhika was good in Ayurveda. She worked in 2 houses as a maid in the morning and in the evening, she worked at a Kerala Ayurvedic Centre for 2 to 3 hours.

Vikram often would get a good 1 hr leg massage done from her, usually on Sundays.

Vikram really admired Radhika's grit and mental strength and her hardworking attitude and would often help her out by paying Advance salaries especially during the school admissions time. He often told her to get Shyam, her husband, to their home but Radhika never dared to do as she knew Vikram would give him a piece of his mind for his irresponsible attitude and callous nature towards his family.

"Has Shyam Bhaiya joined the Toll Naka?" Anjali suddenly asked Radhika. Shyam had managed to find a monitoring job at Toll Naka after quitting his previous desk job and staying at home for almost over a month. The job was to monitor all the incoming and outgoing vehicles and do some tallying and surveillance kind of activity, but it promised him about Rs. 11,000 per month. He had taken the job after repeated arguments with Radhika.

“Yes, he joined day before yesterday, let’s see how long he sticks to it. This time I have given him an ultimatum, if he does anything stupid again, he will have to leave the house.”

“Hahaha, you did a great thing Didi”, Anjali was impressed and appreciated Radhika.

“Then what, Vikram Bhaiyya is right, he is taking things too casually, I cannot handle the entire family on my meagre income. Let him contribute or just get lost” cursed Radhika.

“Chill Didi… Let us hope he takes this job seriously. Don’t worry”, Anjali calmed her.

“Can you please serve lunch to Papa when he is ready to eat. I will just go tell him that I am going to my parents’ house to give them lunch” Anjali added.

Anjali quickly packed the hot Rotis, Rajma chawal, curd and the Sabzi neatly in a 4-tier container and went into Abhay’s room.

“Papa, mummy, and daddy have reached home an hour back. I am taking lunch for them. You please finish lunch once you are ready. I have already told Radhika Didi to keep them ready to be served to you.”

“Don’t worry Beta, I will manage, you please meet your parents. In fact, I would suggest you stay with them for a couple of days." Abhay knew that ever since Sandhya had passed away, not once had Anjali stayed with her parents for more than one day. She was always concerned about his health, his appointments and taking medicines on time. Vikram too helped Abhay with his medical appointments, but he was struggling with his own job, Abhay's health, and his own personal loss.

"No Papa, not now, but I will soon", Anjali smiled confidently. She had seen positive changes in Abhay after his meeting with Shivani and hoped he would soon be the same old self.

Anjali's parents lived in a plush 3 BHK apartment on the 7th floor of a 15 storeyed tower. They were definitely better off than Abhay's family who owned a 2 BHK apartment. But nobody had really bothered about this as both the families had huge respect towards each other. They would often have a get together and night out at both the places.

Sunita answered the door and was overjoyed to see Anjali and gave her a tight hug and a peck on her cheek.

"Mummy, you look tired and seem to have lost a few kgs, have you taken some weight loss program", quipped Anjali.

"Hahaha... I don't need one you know. Your father makes me run here and there. See he has sprained his leg now", Sunita shook her head.

Anjali's father Rajesh gave her dagger looks. "Your mom never gets tired complaining about me.", he argued.

“Papa, you need to be careful, you are not some 35-year-old action hero now doing silly stunts.”, Anjali scolded him.

“Let us eat now, we are too hungry. What have you prepared?”, Rajesh changed the topic.

“Sure Papa, I will quickly arrange everything on the table for all of us.”

“By the way, did you pray for all of us in Amritsar”, Anjali teased her mother.

“Of course, we asked for a cute little cuddly grandchild to keep us busy and fulfil all its tantrums”, Sunita blurted out and Anjali’s expressions changed.

CHAPTER 10. THE STRETCH

Vikram alighted from the cramped autorickshaw and heaved a sigh of relief. He then looked at his watch and groaned. He quickened his pace for the next 80 odd steps until he reached the grand entrance gate of his office. He quickly drew his tattered ID card and flashed it at the security guard before swiping at the entry gates which looked similar to the ones used in the Metro stations.

He checked the time again. It was 9.45am just in time for the 10am client meeting. Today his boss had asked all the team members to reach office sharp before the meeting as it was going to be a historic one, he had exclaimed. For Vikram, every meeting seemed monotonous; the initial 10 mins of the meetings only made sense to him and rest of it all were only a repetition. Finally, it always ended up with the boss giving some dramatic account of the way his previous team was always motivated and the way they stretched day and night to perform at their best and won the customer delight award. 'Bullshit!' He almost always would mutter to himself after the meeting was over. These bosses know quite well to extract work by putting fake pressures and when it came to appreciation, hog all the limelight and all that the juniors would get is a general one liner appreciation addressed to the team.

And of course, when it came to the yearly appraisals, they would act as if you were a stranger to them. He had seen 5 appraisals now and each one was no different from the previous one. It would always boil down to 'You are no doubt an extremely critical team member and have always done what was expected from you, but what we want is you running the extra mile and doing something innovative for the organisation to soar to new heights.' Vikram would patiently nod his head and wait for the feedback session to get over.

Vikram reached the aesthetically supreme lobby of his building and waited for the lift. The lobby was no less than a five-star hotel reception area. His organisation had state of the art infrastructure and always pumped in more money for the enhancing the same. This was a ploy to attract more clients by impressing them with a guided tour of the entire property and show off the workforce and the infrastructure they possessed for executing the delivery operations.

Vikram wished that in addition to this grandeur, had they given timely promotions to the employees and not been too stingy on the yearly increments, they could have had a better control on their employee attrition rates. In the corporate world, it was all about being a useful 'Resource', once your utilisation is over, you are just cast away, from one project to another project or perhaps even ousted from the company if you fail to fit into their vision.

His Offshore Development Centre or ODC as it was commonly known was located on the 3rd floor. He kept his bag on his desk and quickly went to freshen himself up. He had a comb, facewash, sanitiser, and a bottle of deodorant in his desk drawer. These were very much required after traveling by the crowded Mumbai local trains.

"Vikram, the boss is calling all of us to assemble in Conference Room 8", his teammate and cubicle partner Sandeep shouted. The meeting went on for a good one and half hours and by the time, they all were out, they were all sombre looking with every ounce of energy sucked out from them. It turned out that 3 to 4 critical bugs had been found in two of the modules during the User Acceptance testing phase and hence their planned application Go-Live date had to be delayed by at least 2 weeks.

The client did not take this well and had given a good rough edge of his tongue especially to the boss who did not utter anything until the end of the meeting where he committed to the rest of the action points that he was going to undertake and get all the issues resolved.

Vikram was luckily not involved directly in the said modules, but Sandeep had to take the full blow. He felt sorry for Sandeep.

"Don't worry mate, you will resolve them asap and push them forward", Vikram comforted his pal. "As they say shit happens, all the time.", Sandeep groaned.

Vikram gave him a sympathetic look and unlocked his desktop machine. He had just started going through his emails when another email popped up in the notification bar. It was a one-to-one email addressed to him by his boss. "Vikram, want to speak to you about today's meeting."

He knew what was coming at him next. He quietly went to his boss's cabin and waited.

"Vikram, did you see the way we were all embarrassed by the client today. One of these days, I am going to lose it on Sandeep and get him fired. This is just not acceptable.", he fumed.

"But Sir, Sandeep has worked really hard, and it is just that he had overlooked a couple of things." Vikram dared.

"Vikram, do you even know what you are talking? We just can't justify this", the boss exploded. "Now listen carefully, I know that even if you are not responsible for the Report module, you can easily analyse the root cause and fix it, so I want you to immediately start working on it and try to resolve all of them by end of tomorrow."

"But Sir, I have already got too many things on my plate. I have to complete the architecture design for the new application that we discussed" Vikram started to protest but his boss cut him off.

"Put all that on hold, just sit with Sandeep and fix these on priority." He commanded.

Vikram stormed out of the cabin cursing and threw his notebook on the desk.

"What did the Hitler say now", Sandeep wanted to know.

"He wants me to just shove off all my urgent work aside and help your team fix the issues by end of tomorrow. You know that means we will have to stay the night today and complete", Vikram sighed.

Sandeep was inwardly grateful to his boss as he knew that with Vikram around, he could quickly fix them and be done with this as early as possible. But he genuinely felt sorry for Vikram.

"Well, pal, I have got some good news for you to make you forget this shit. Diya is coming next week to India. She will be working from here for a week."

Vikram almost fell from his chair. Diya was his bestie in office who had shifted to USA a couple of years ago. He had not met her after that. She was not in close contact with him either. But they did exchange messages and greetings once in a blue moon.

"What are you saying? Why suddenly here? She did not tell me." Vikram said blankly.

"Maybe she wanted to surprise you, but I played spoilers", Sandeep smiled.

Sandeep knew Vikram and Diya were really good friends and would mostly hang around with each other in office. They would work late till night on many days, have dinner and go home together. Diya stayed 3 to 4 stops before Vikram's house, and they would take the same route company bus in the morning as well as in the night. They helped each other mutually and managed to deliver extra ordinarily in their project activities. They even implemented couple of innovations in their projects with each other's help and saved some revenue for their respective clients. But now all that seemed to be a different lifetime.

"Come Sandy, let us go to the pantry and have a cup of Green Tea, I desperately need one. We have a tough day ahead."

Vikram remembered what Sandhya always used to tell him, "When things are too much for you to handle, just let them float for a while. Refresh and Resume." He was missing his mom today more than ever.

CHAPTER 11. THE CONCERT

Ajay rang the bell twice before it was opened by Anjali. “Hey Bhabhi, is Abhay Sir all set for today?”, Ajay enquired.

“He has been a nervous wreck since last night; and at the same time, he is confident of what he is going to play”, replied to Anjali. “Guess he is waiting to give his best”, she added with a smile.

Abhay stepped out from his room in a turquoise-coloured kurta and white pyjamas. “Welcome Ajay! Man, you have got me in such a muddle…You shared the video and look at my condition now!” Abhay expressed with a mock anger in his tone.

“Yes Sir, because of that I got to know that you look charismatic in traditional!” smiled Ajay with raised eyebrows. Anjali joined them both and giggled listening to them.

“Good morning, Ajay! Papa, how are you going to travel with the tabla? Shall I arrange a cab?” enquired Vikram as he joined them for the breakfast.

“I will drop him, Vikram. Will I also get to hear you papa?” Anjali’s question made Vikram think on joining her if they are allowed to attend the program.

“No beta, this is just an introduction session of our batch. Every year they celebrate an annual day function for which families will be invited”, Abhay said which hinted that he will surely participate in the Annual Day program.

“Bhaiya, Bhabhi, I’ll make a move. Just dropped in to wish Sir; I need to go to the studio and help Aunty with the arrangements. Bye Sir. All the best! See you there.” Ajay got up from the sofa and moved towards the door.

“Thank you my dear! Yes, meet you there”, Abhay waved at him.

“Bye Ajay!” called out Vikram and signalled him to shoot a video while Abhay performs.

Ajay nodded his head in full enthusiasm and smiled at him. Deep down Vikram’s heart, he wished to be like Ajay who was always full of life. Ajay found happiness in the smallest of the small things and always looked contended. He looked equally comfortable spending time with people of any age-group unlike Vikram who felt irked to move out of his comfort-zone and his set of known people.

“Papa which song are you going to play?” Vikram asked while he packed his lunch box.

“I am going to play Raag Khamaj as it keeps the mood light and seems perfect for the introduction session” Abhay spoke and hummed the Raag.

Vikram nodded his head in agreement; he also knew Abhay chose Raag Khamaj as it was Sandhya’s favourite Raag. He slipped his feet inside his formal shoes and spoke, “Good choice Papa…All the best! Bye. Bye Anjali”.

Anjali waved at him, looked at Abhay and said, “Papa give me 20 minutes, I’ll get ready and then let’s proceed.”

Abhay nodded and went back to his room; he packed his Tabla and Gedi (cloth ring on top of which the drums are placed; these are used as a support for the drums while playing) in a cloth -case while Anjali got ready.

She soon raced towards him holding the car keys, "Ready Papa? Shall we leave?". He nodded and carried his Tabla carefully and stepped out of his room. She silently prayed for his program to be loved by all as they left for the venue.

They soon reached 'Just Be There'. Anjali called Ajay and asked him to come down to help Abhay carry the Tabla and his bag. "Ajay do not forget to record his program and thank you", Anjali spoke as she handed Abhay's bag to Ajay. Ajay gave a thumbs up and said, "I will take care of everything."

Abhay checked the batch and program-list; there were 15 people in the batch, and he realised that everyone had to showcase their talents. The first performer was a 65-year-old lady who was also a Kathak dancer. Her performance and her grace soon made her everyone's favourite. The second one was a 25-year-old young man who amazed everyone with his art of beatboxing.

Abhay soon felt a wave of panic hit him from within and he rushed outside the room, seeing this, Shivani followed him quickly and faced him. "Are you alright, Abhay?", she was concerned.

"I don't think I am in a position to perform now. I will not be able to face the audience." Abhay was sweating profusely. She picked a glass of lemonade which was kept at the refreshment corner and handed it to him.

"You will be alright. Don't worry; I am there with you; Just go to the stage and perform. Consider it as your first step in your duty towards your family; you are going to dedicate it to Sandhya. Just imagine how proud she would feel to see you perform."

Abhay took her words in hungrily. He knew he desperately needed to hear such soothing words. He stepped back into the room with renewed vigour. He placed his Tabla on the Gedi and faced the audience…suddenly a nostalgic wave rippled in his mind. Once on stage, as a true artist, his confidence increased and he began, "Good morning, friends! I'll be presenting raag Khamaj; A lot many ghazals and thumris are composed in this raag because of its ability to keep the mood light." He played a piece which showcased the beauty of the Shuddha Nishad note in the ascent and Komala Nishad note in the descent.

Shivani gave a standing ovation and requested him to play Tabla while she sang P*ayoji Meine Ram Ratan Dhan Payo-* a Meera bhajan based on the same Raga. Though she sang the first 2 lines alone, she was joined by all the members of the batch by the time the second paragraph ended. It was rendered beautifully as if they had practised together. They then decided to sing *Vaishnava Jana To* as they wanted to stay in the same raga. This time two more instrument players from the Staff joined on the Violin and the Morsing.

By the end of the program, everyone seemed to be comfortable with each other; every single person in the batch was coming out of the cocoon by fighting some stage of depression under Shivani's guidance.

"Wow, Abhay you rocked the concert today", applauded Shivani when they gathered for the lunch break.

"Shivani, I never knew you are such a beautiful singer. Thank you for singing one of Sandhya's favourite songs. It was sort of a nice feeling to connect with everyone musically", Abhay spoke as he carefully placed the *phulkas* in his plate.

Shivani smiled and added, "Enjoy the lunch! I'll catch up with other members too". As she started moving away, she felt he had something to say to her which made her turn back to look at him and Abhay added, "It was only because you gave me the required courage that I could face everyone and perform", Abhay had a look of gratitude on his face. Shivani just winked at him and left.

Anjali was feeling a bit relaxed seeing the men of the house get better with their moods. She now decided to talk to Vikram about the frequently asked question by others to her.

CHAPTER 12: THE EVASIVE

"Are you going to decide with Vikram on this or shall we speak to him?" Sunita's words ringed in her ears. Anjali tried concentrating on the novel she was reading but her thoughts kept going back to the same topic which had irked her that day when she had visited her parents.

Anjali's parents were not the dominating or interfering type, but they genuinely felt their daughter must take some firm decision and as all parents, they wanted their daughter to enjoy motherhood. She had been married for almost 3 years now. Sandhya's demise had put a break in their plans but now it had been more than a year. They felt it was time for them to move ahead and also believed that a baby coming home will greatly help in alleviating their pain and give them new motivation in life. But both Anjali and Vikram had avoided this subject for a long time. Eventually Anjali had also come around, but it was Vikram who was not ready. They had spoken a couple of times on this, and Vikram had become restless, and this had led to arguments between them. Vikram was still not out completely from Sandhya's demise and though he was working out his own life he still was not ready for such a big decision. Anjali had decided to wait patiently as she knew eventually Vikram would also be ready for this.

But now a ray of hope had filled Anjali as she witnessed the changes in Abhay after he had joined Shivani's yoga studio. He had become more occupied than before and as a result, his moods remained stable, and he also seemed physically recovering. Vikram had been happier to see Abhay recovering and his mood was also light.

Anjali watched the video for the 3rd time which Ajay had shared on Abhay's tabla performance in the concert earlier that day. It seemed to be flawless. She was really happy and relieved seeing Abhay getting back his focus on his favourite hobbies.

She had immediately forwarded it to Vikram but got a response from him after an hour.

"Just watched the video. Wow, dad seems to rock the concert. Very good ??", Vikram had texted back. Anjali was excited now. "Can you come home early, or I mean by the correct time?", Anjali asked.

"Sure, will try, anyway I fixed all of Sandy's issues last night and the boss is also relieved, so I definitely deserve that break. I will try to leave by 7pm.But again, can't guarantee anything. Ok TTYL, have a meeting now." Vikram replied back in text.

"Ok...sure...bye", Anjali wrote and started back to the page she had left in the novel.

Abhay had reached home after the concert, and he seemed to be too tired but still there was a contentment in his face after such a long time. It was 4.30 in the afternoon. Anjali prepared a strong ginger tea for him. He slowly started sipping the ginger tea relishing the aroma.

"This is really soothing beta", he thanked Anjali who smiled back.

"This is the 5th time I am seeing the video Papa, you were too good in the concert", she praised him with a big smile.

Abhay was surprised. “What! You have the video, is it? Ajay has shared with you! he didn’t even tell me about it”, Abhay made a face.

“Hahaha, I had only told him that I will show you the video myself so that you can see for yourself how well you have performed, and I can see your expressions while seeing the video”, Anjali grinned.

Abhay nodded. Whatever makes you happy. “Have you sent it to Vikram?”, he wanted to know. “Yes, Papa, he was quite impressed and proud of you, he said he will get Rasmalai for you from Majedaar Mishtan”, Anjali told him.

Vikram and Anjali knew that Abhay was fond of Rasmalai, especially the ones prepared in his favourite sweet shop, Majedaar Mishtan; but he had forgotten all about it in the last one year.

“You remember how me, and Sandhya used to attack the Rasmalai, we literally used to compete to get them first and gulp.”, Abhay reminisced.

“Yes, and Mummyji would always get the better of you. More than the taste of the Rasmalai, she used to relish the look on your face when you lost that extra piece to her”, laughed Anjali, filled with nostalgia.

Both of them laughed at this and then smiled to themselves. Abhay then retired to his room as he wanted to take a power nap while Anjali decided to buy some vegetables and fruits from the nearby market.

It was 8.30pm when Vikram reached home. He had brought the Rasmalai as promised and all the three soon enjoyed a warm supper and a great dessert. They talked about Abhay's performance in the concert as well as Vikram's appreciation by the boss for fixing all the issues quickly.

Once they had all retired to their rooms, Anjali got anxious yet excited. It was time to bring in the topic. Vikram did seem to be in a relaxed mood.

"You know, the other day, when I went to meet my parents, mom raised the topic of planning our kid.", Anjali blurted out. Vikram's expression changed suddenly.

"You know Anjali, I am not ready for it, and we have already spoken about it.", Vikram was irked.

"I did not bring this up, you know this very well, but we cannot shut others, as a parent, they are genuinely concerned for us. They feel that if we have a baby, then everyone in the house would come alive and forget their troubles. Even Papa will be occupied." She said plainly.

"Anju, you know it has just been over a year since mom left us. I still cannot bring myself to think about a baby. I don't blame your parents or anybody, but how can I just get on like that and enjoy life, I miss her so much and Papa is also depressed. Can't we talk about this later, right now I am tired and want to get some sleep", Vikram evaded her and got ready to sleep.

Anjali knew it was futile and did not want to press further. She started getting ready to sleep but knew she would not be able to sleep that easily.

Both Vikram and Anjali were silently thinking about the same topic, but they were unaware that Abhay had listened to every word of it now, although he did not mean to eavesdrop, he had just chanced upon to their room and then been party to this conversation.

Abhay retired to his room silently and looked at Sandhya's photo. He had tears in his eyes. 'My poor kids!! What are they going through because of me!! He felt guilty more than anything now.'

"Sandhya, I am so sorry, I have not been taking care of our kids. See what Vikram is saying, he does not want to live his life happily. If I had been strong enough, I could have shown him the right way. Anjali has been patiently suppressing her desire to become a mother, she has not raised it till date in front of me just because I have been weak and lost in my own world.

Shivani was right. I have no right to make the living suffer just because someone dear to me left me. And of course, you never really left me, you are always around me everywhere.

Why could I not understand this? But Sandhya, I promise you this. I will bring Vikram and Anjali together and make them live again. I don't know how but, I will take Shivani's help; She will definitely have a solution to this."

CHAPTER 13. THE OFFER

"I am feeling very guilty of making my children suffer because of my selfishness and weakness", Abhay lamented as he narrated the entire conversation of Vikram and Anjali which he had accidently overheard. He paused for a while when the waiter approached their table with their orders. Shivani had ordered a lemonade while Abhay settled for a cold coffee. Abhay had called Shivani the very next morning after the incident for an advance appointment. She had suggested to meet at a café near her studio as her room in the studio was undergoing some upkeeps and their next session was four days away.

She took a sip of lemonade and spoke, "Abhay, it is never too late to realise one's folly and take a corrective action. You never did anything wrong to hurt anyone deliberately. It is said that when the right time arrives, things start to fall automatically in place. So, don't keep on self-inflicting yourself and giving yourself more pain. It does not help you in anyway.

You have a few additional responsibilities now; make sure to take out time and talk to Vikram. Let him vent out his boxed emotions. You both have successfully been dodging Sandhya's topic, with each other, ever since she left you; by whatever background information you gave, I strongly feel there is a sort of an invisible thin wall between you and Vikram.

You both are bound to each other by Sandhya and now you do not know what to say to each other. Since you are his father,

Vikram needs you to back him up and give him the fatherly support as well as the friendly shoulders which he is craving for.

Why don't you two go out somewhere together and recreate the amazing father-son bond that you used to share before? Talk about this to Anjali; she will be able to help you decide on this plan further".

"Shivani, why didn't I think of this before, it sounds to be a great idea", marvelled Abhay at Shivani's ease of providing solutions.

Shivani felt a happy breeze around her to see her patient improving and trying to improve other's life too. She leaned back on the chair, rested her back, nodded her head and said, "Let us help one more person to step out of the cocoon but this time I'm involved in an indirect way".

They both finished their drinks and Shivani asked Abhay to join her to check her studio before leaving home.

"This arrangement is better than the previous one, isn't it?", Abhay asked looking at the temporary arrangement of the couches which were shifted near to the right-side wall. She appreciated his skill to check these nuances and said, "Let us maintain it this way, this looks more spacious."

The maintenance work was almost done, Shivani signed a few papers and completed paying the bills and requested the watchman to turn off the lights, fans and lock the studio before going back home.

“Abhay, I want to ask you some favour if you don’t mind”, Shivani said hesitantly.

Abhay was surprised. What favour could he possibly do to Shivani who was much stronger and more stable than him?

“Actually, I want to use your skills more to my studio’s advantage. I know I am being little selfish here. We could jointly work in the studio to make things more systematic, and I could even utilise your experiencing of teaching and organising stuff. It is just a proposition; I will pay you too; There is no compulsion on this; It is completely your call”, so saying Shivani started her car.

“Come on Abhay, let me drop you home.” She changed the topic.

“Shivani, I really don’t know what to say, your offer is really good, but will I be able to do justice, that I am really not sure”, Abhay replied as he got into the car seat next to her.

“Let me sort out my personal problems first and then I will think about your offer”.

Shivani smiled and nodded. She knew that it was not easy for Abhay to simply get on with new stuff but was confident that soon things will change for the positive.

They soon arrived outside the society where Abhay lived.

“Why don’t you come home Shivani?”, Abhay offered. But Shivani declined saying that she had to rush home for some personal work, but she promised that she would definitely plan it for the next time.

Abhay was patiently waiting for Vikram to arrive from office and soon the trio joined for dinner.

"What is the matter, Vikram, you look too tired?", Anjali was concerned.

"Oh, it is nothing, there was too much crowd everywhere today, especially the trains today, supposedly a couple of trains were cancelled, and the platform was completely crowded. Somehow reached home but they literally ironed me out", Vikram was complaining.

"Vikram, I was thinking why don't we go to Health-Freaks this Saturday. It has been ages since we went". He was referring to the club where they both used to often go and play Table Tennis, Badminton and sometimes swim.

"Ohh...hmm… I am not sure, Papa, let us see, maybe we could actually…", Vikram was considering it more now.

"It is fine beta if you don't feel like it, I will plan some other time", Abhay started to say but Vikram shook his head. "I am actually thinking now that we should go. After all, I have lost touch and need a shot on the table tennis."

"And of course, I will get a break from you both and could use a little privacy time for myself. I am actually thinking of getting a spa and salon appointment.", Anjali echoed and gave a thumbs-up.

"Very good idea. Anju beta, I suggest that you visit your parents too and perhaps you can have lunch with them, we both will have lunch at Bala's".

Bala's was a South Indian restaurant which served unlimited Thali which aroused Abhay's taste buds. It was a favourite spot for Abhay and Sandhya who often would relish the thali especially the unbeatable sambhar and rasam which it offered. Vikram had also accompanied them several times even though he was not a great fan of the thali, but he enjoyed the kheer very much which was served at the end.

After Abhay went to his room to take his medicines, Vikram and Anjali looked at each other.

"Did you notice the changes in him? He wants to play badminton and table-tennis with you." Anjali smiled.

"Yeah, I was quite surprised. It is a good sign though. I am sort of feeling relieved now.", Vikram agreed.

"You know what, we should ask him to resume college too. That will keep him occupied", Anjali suggested.

"Nah, I don't think it is a good idea right now. He is still taking those sleeping pills and anti-depressants. We need to make him stop that, first."

"You are right, let him take his own sweet time. Shivani Ma'am will take good care of him.", Anjali said with a twinkle in her eyes.

CHAPTER 14. THE PERSPECTIVE

The Skype messenger on his office desktop popped up a message with a familiar picture. "Hey wassup, Vicky", Diya had pinged.

"Hey, long time. how you doing?", Vikram replied back.

"Guess where I am now" Diya put up a smiley.

Vikram knew she had reached Mumbai and must have come to office already.

"USA, right? Must be pretty late there now", Vikram continued to pretend.

"Hahaha… I am in Mumbai yaar. In office now."

"Ohh nice. You did not tell me. Just surprised me completely." Vikram smirked to himself.

"That was the whole intention ??Anyways, I am here only for a week and will be coming to office only today and tomorrow, later I will be working from home. Have to visit Shirdi as well, so it is a very tight schedule for me." Diya said.

"Ok. Then we can meet today for lunch. Tomorrow, we have a team lunch and other meetings so won't be possible for me to meet you." Vikram replied.

"Sure, it is 12 noon. How about 1pm for lunch? I have meetings from half past two" Diya asked.

"Perfect, see you at 1 pm", Vikram agreed.

He reached the cafeteria at 12.50 P.M., since it became too crowded during the peak time from 1 to 2 pm, it was very difficult to find seats. The cafeteria was one among its kind; It was very huge and had different options for lunch. There were different outlets which served various cuisines.

Initially, it had been exciting to explore each food, but now it had become the same monotonous and boring stuff. Vikram generally brought lunch box from home but once or twice a week, he would eat at the cafeteria.

He felt a sharp tap on his head from behind and whirled around. "What the hell?", he started to say when he noticed a blond girl with sunglasses smiling at him. He failed to recognise her for a moment as she removed her sunglasses and winked at him.

"Diya...!!! you look completely different; for a second I thought it is some foreign client", Vikram was shocked as he shook hands with her. Diya had undergone a makeover and styled herself for a blonde look. She was wearing a formal shirt and trouser.

"Hahaha… even my manager said the same thing. but you still look the same Vicky, except that you seem to have lost a few pounds and have grown a bit older too", she giggled as she sat opposite to him.

"So how are Raj and Ritvaan doing?", enquired Vikram, referring to Diya's husband and her 2-year-old son.

"You didn't ask how I am doing. They are all fine. Ritvaan has become very naughty and tears the house down. I have left him at Mamma's house today."

"Oh nice. And sorry, how are you doing?", Vikram smiled.

"Yeah, life is on. Just balancing work and home. Work has become boring too; nothing much to learn. Been doing the same kind of stuff since last 2 years.", Diya shrugged." How is your dad now and Anjali?"

"All fine. anyway, I will go order food now." Vikram said and got up.

"You want me to come along?" Diya asked.

"Nope, please save the seats, it will get too crowded now and I don't want to lose these seats. I know what to order for us.", he smiled.

Diya got a call from Raj and got busy while Vikram went to the counter and started to order. It took quite some time, but finally, he came with a large tray which had 4 -5 hot phulkas, one bowl of Bhindi Kurkure, a bowl of Jeera rice and yet another containing piping hot butter Dal Fry. He placed them on the table carefully.

"Wow! My favourite! I was missing these for so long", squealed Diya with delight, while taking in the fragrance of the mouth-watering food.

Vikram giggled and went to get plates and spoons for both of them. They started their food and Diya hungrily gorged on the Bhindi Kurkure. "Heavenly, the same old taste, thank you so much Vicky", she smiled.

Diya observed that though Vikram was talking, still he was not the same old self. There was something amiss.

“So how is the USA? Are you guys planning to permanently settle down there or what?”, Vikram asked.

“I really don’t know, sometimes I feel like it, but I really miss India and feel like coming back. How about you Vicky, are you not planning for any onsite opportunities?”.

“Nope, I am quite fine with being here. Moreover, dad’s health issues are there; and Anjali works at an old age Home, so we are all tied here, plus I don’t feel like going anywhere outside to settle down.”

“What about your future plans? When are you planning a baby?”, Diya asked, and Vikram felt a bit uncomfortable.

“Diya, you know that mom passed away last year. It has been quite tough for all of us. Dad has been under depression and undergoing treatments. So, I am still not ready for such a big decision.” Vikram replied.

“I know, Vicky, and I am really sorry about your mom. But it has been more than a year now. You guys need to start living your lives; And have you thought about Anjali? What is her fault? Even she must be desiring to have a kid and experience motherhood. Have you both discussed about it?”

“Yes, we have had arguments, in fact, 2 days back her parents had started the same topic”. Vikram sounded weak.

“See Vicky, I know it is tough for you and you will always miss your mom. But let me tell you something…I have been recently reading a book written by Dr. Brian Weiss. You must have heard about him. He is a famous American psychiatrist, hypnotherapist, and author who specializes in past lives and related stuff.

He says that the people who are very close to us always find a way to come back to us in some or the other forms. Like, for example, your father in some previous life was your grandson or your wife in a previous life must have been your daughter or even a friend.

So why don't you consider it this way. Since your mom loves you so much, she perhaps could be wanting to come back to you all, maybe as your child. And right now, you are not giving her that opportunity? Just think about it. This is just my perspective and ultimately it is your call and Anjali's too", Diya spoke solemnly and looked at Vikram's eyes which were a bit moist now.

CHAPTER 15. THE BONDING

"Papa, 0-3…good going", Vikram cheered Abhay while he geared up for the next serve. "Thanks…But what happened to you? Come on, charge up", Abhay called out to his son while he stepped forward for a back-hand shot.
They rallied continuously for around 3 minutes when Vikram finally took his first point. "Yes! Finally, 1-3 papa… 3-1… your serve!" Vikram said while he passed the table tennis ball to Abhay.

They had a great match; Abhay won by two points in the first set and Vikram took lead in the second set and won by 5 points. Both were completely exhausted and drenched in sweat and it seemed their arms and legs were tearing apart.

"I am too tired and getting cramps everywhere", Vikram groaned, and Abhay agreed by saying, "Yeah, me too. It has been ages since we played last time. We are quite out of touch."
They took a break after the match and proceeded to the eatery outlet in the club which served fresh juices and some healthy snacks.

Vikram ordered a cup of buttered salted corn and 2 glasses of lemonade for them, and proceeded towards the pool-facing table where Abhay was sitting and looking at the group of kids enjoying their pool-time with their parents.

"Ah! Vikram…do you remember we used to visit this place almost every weekend during your summer vacation?" Abhay told without turning his attention from the pool. "Yes papa! And the first time you taught me table tennis was in this club…what a great time we had! You remember Ma had left for some conference in Delhi for 2 weeks? And we partied here one whole day and then continued the party at home…still remember how it had made her jealous of all the fun that she had missed", Vikram laughed remembering the day and simultaneously sipping his lemonade.

Abhay turned his attention from the lively swimming pool and looked at Vikram, held his hand and said, "Vicky, we both have been holding up a lot of things from each other, I feel it is high time that we both let out everything. Sandhya was, is and always will be a guide to us.

We have learnt a lot from her; Time management, personal and professional life balance; her lively nature and her patience. We need to take her memories in our stride and live our lives fruitfully", Abhay paused to look at Vikram's reaction. He was listening to Abhay but feared to make an eye contact lest he will end up crying; Vikram kept stirring his juice and tried to say something, but the words got choked in his throat.

"Beta, shall we go to our room? I'll inform them to get the juice glasses and corn to our room", Abhay spoke as he got up from his chair. Vikram nodded his head as Abhay proceeded to spell out his request to the concerned people. The lush green club which had a lot of activity divisions, had a party hall which was big enough to accommodate 200 people. They had about 15 rooms for the guests whenever there were any events conducted. In case of no booking for any function, these rooms were made available for the regular club visitors who were allowed to book a room from 10am to 6pm and enjoy the club activities at their own pace.

Once in every 2 months, the Singhs used to book a room, based on the availability, in the green-house club and enjoy the full day playing all the activities in the club and relaxing along the poolside.

Vikram walked towards the balcony and stood there holding the railing. The balcony faced the lawn-tennis court. The coach was training his students and there was a lot of action going on in the tennis court as well as inside Vikram's heart.

Abhay collected the snack tray from the waiter, thanked him and placed the tray on the table, walked towards the balcony and placed his hand on Vikram's shoulder and said, "Beta, have the corn; I know you love to eat that hot…it has already become warm."

Vikram turned and clung to Abhay for some time just as he would do when he was a small boy. Abhay hugged him tightly. "Sorry papa, I tried to make myself believe that I am very strong and avoided talking about Ma and in the process drifted away from you and Anjali. I was afraid of opening up and crying in front of you as I feared you will further break down. You already have suffered a lot of Papa", he sobbed.

Abhay blinked back some tears and said, "I failed to be a pillar of strength to you and Anjali. I'm sorry Vikram; Sandhya has left a deep void in us. We both got so lost in our own world that we did not think a bit about Anjali. Let us make up for that. Make sure to keep Anjali happy; don't worry about me…I have realised my folly and now I will come out strong with all of your support and Shivani's guidance.

You have the entire life to live, this is just the start where you and Anjali, as a young couple, must understand one another, live your life to the fullest and build a strong relation with each other. Actually, Vikram, you both will be celebrating your 3rd wedding anniversary next month. And I want you to take Anjali somewhere on a holiday. I want you both to spend some quality time with each other. I have wanted to talk to you about this for some time; The time has come to take some decisions. You and Anjali should start planning for a kid now that is if you both have a plan to experience parenthood."

"Papa, you remember what Ma used to say when she was a having a tough time at office and you used to tell her to quit the job, she would say that she will take retirement only when she is blessed with a grandchild so that there will be someone to keep her busy at home all time. Now she is not there to play with my child." Vikram could not control his tears.

"I know beta…me and Sandhya had planned of so many things that we will do together for our grandchild, all the games and stories that we will teach and the songs we will sing. But I will do all that now; I will be your child's grandpa as well as grandma. I will make up for Sandhya's absence. We all will live cherishing her thought every single day… but we will not lead a life that causes grief to others."

"Papa, you know what my friend Diya said the other day? She says that people who are very close to us always find a way to come back in our lives, in different forms. Do you really think Ma will come back to us as my baby?" Vikram asked Abhay with fervour.

"Yes beta, I am inclined to believe in what Diya says."

Abhay's words boosted Vikram and he felt that he had to speak with Anjali but in his own style. He decided that he will plan a big surprise holiday for Anjali for their 3rd anniversary and that is where he will start afresh.

Vikram and Abhay freshened up at the club and proceeded to have lunch at Bala's. They relived all their memories with Sandhya at the restaurant and relished the food like the way they used to do before.

Vikram called Anjali and told her that they were coming to pick her up from her parents' house. Anjali could tell from Vikram's tone that he and Abhay had spent quality time with each other just as she had hoped.

The rest of the day was spent with Anjali's parents and Abhay slept that night peacefully but not before thanking Sandhya. He also dropped a "Thank You" message to Shivani and told her that he would fill her in with the details in their next session.

CHAPTER 16. THE SURPRISE

Abhay reached 'Just Be There' studio at sharp 9 am for his session with Shivani. He was quite excited to share the moments she had with Vikram and how they bonded well and decided to start things afresh.

However, his excitement turned into disappointment when the receptionist told him that Shivani had to cancel today's session with him as she got an urgent call from a friend who had to be hospitalised. She had asked the receptionist to convey the message to Abhay and had asked him to continue with his regular Yoga Asanas and meditation practices. She would soon fix another appointment with him.

Abhay proceeded towards his Yoga room where his other batchmates had already gathered and were readying their Yoga mats to just start off their daily routine of pranayam and other Asanas subsequently.

Abhay picked up his spot next to Mr. Malhotra who gave him a warm smile and they all soon got completely focussed with their Yoga session and by the time they had completed all of their designated practice, it was almost 10.30 am.

Abhay picked up his accessories and packed his bag and headed towards the exit when the receptionist beckoned to him.

'Abhay Sir, Shivani Madam is on the line. She was just enquiring about you, and you arrived.' She winked at Abhay who smiled.

"Hey Abhay, I just had to rush at the last moment as one of my friends got food poisoned and had to be hospitalised. I am really sorry that I had to cancel your session today." Shivani apologised.

"No problem, Shivani, that was more important and our session could wait. By the way, how is your friend now?", Abhay asked with genuine concern.

"She is fine now Abhay, thanks, luckily, they brought her on time otherwise her condition would have worsened. Doctor has given her an injection and a few medicines as well as diet schedule. She will be alright and discharged today itself. I am currently at the Jeevan Mitr hospital."

"Oh okay, actually, that is not far from here, do you mind if I just drop in there for some time? We can meet at the Navratna restaurant just adjacent to the hospital.", Abhay was hesitant, but he thought it could not hurt to ask.

"Umm well, actually, it is a good idea because my friend is sleeping now and it will take some time for her to wake up, so we can just catch up for an hour. I did not have breakfast today and getting hunger pangs.", Shivani complained.

Abhay took an auto rickshaw from the studio and after around 15 mins he reached the restaurant. He called Shivani and she came down from the hospital building and waved.

They found a comfortable place to sit and settled down.

"I hope I did not bother you Shivani by asking to meet me here." Abhay was feeling awkward.

“No not at all, Abhay, in fact, I must thank you. I was getting nauseated by the hospital smell, I don’t quite like those, but I had to visit my friend. She is actually a loner and her maid brought her here. Anyway, how was your time with Vikram? Did you guys finally empty all your suppressed emotions to each other?”

Abhay narrated all the events that transpired between the two of them the day before and Shivani patiently listened to each and every bit of it giving a look of appreciation to Abhay.

“See Abhay, didn’t I tell you that by communicating clearly and sincerely, you both will be able to break the thin walls that you had created between the two of you. Vikram may be grown up, but he is still a kid in front of you and you did right by being his father and his friend too. I am really happy that things worked well for you, and I am sure he and Anjali will soon take a positive decision favourable to the three of you.”

“I must really thank you Shivani for your support and guidance”, Abhay said.

“Let us order something now, I am starving”, Shivani laughed.

“I had breakfast at home so I will settle for a cup of Masala Tea. You must try the Onion Tomato Uthappam here. They taste awesome”, Abhay suggested.

“Oh, is it, I have not tried, so will go with your suggestion”, Shivani agreed and placed the order. As Abhay had said, they tasted really nice, and Shivani enjoyed every morsel of it.

“Shivani, as I will be completing my sessions with you by next week…I was thinking of accepting the offer you made the other day…it will keep me occupied", Abhay said carefully choosing the words, as they left the restaurant. Shivani was thrilled with this news and said, "That is a great decision Abhay, and I am really looking forward to working with you".

"Same here", Abhay said, and she proceeded back to the hospital while he left for home.

Vikram reached home in the evening a bit earlier which pleasantly surprised Abhay and Anjali. He asked Anjali to check the file in his bag while he went inside to freshen up.

Anjali wondered what the file could be, started to open it and it read-

Dear Anju, as it is our 3rd wedding anniversary next month, I have planned for a vacation to Malaysia with you. I have already applied for leave and it has been approved too.

The file had tentative details about day wise itinerary for 6 days and Vikram had meticulously planned and listed out all the must visit places that they would be covering.

She looked up from the file to see both father and son grinning at each other.

"Papa, you knew this and didn't even tell me?", she asked with a surprised tone.

"If I had told you beforehand, we would have missed your priceless reaction", Abhay replied seeing her happy reaction.

"Papa, will you be able to manage alone when we are going out? I'll ask Radhika to cook the meals and serve the breakfast too; please take your medicines regularly…and…'

Abhay cut Anjali halfway "Beta, do not worry…I'll take care of myself. By the way, I forgot to tell you both, Shivani has offered me a job in the Studio. We both have some plans and need to work on how we go about implementing it, so I am going to be too busy in the coming weeks", he chuckled.

Vikram and Anjali were pleased on hearing this. "Superb, Papa, you will do great", they both hugged him.

CHAPTER 17. THE ANNIVERSARY

Three weeks had passed since Abhay had accepted Shivani's offer in her venture and guide students. His own formal sessions with her had long been completed. It had brought out many positive changes in Abhay and had given him a new perspective of life. It had broadened his outlook towards others and made him more sensitive towards other people's struggles and needs.

He was working on his laptop at home and finalizing the plans for the seminar that he was going to conduct in his own college where he had quit his regular professor job.

He was, of course, not going to resume his college job but he thought it was a nice way to interact with his old peers and his students through this platform from time to time. His college Dean had readily agreed to his idea and was happy for Abhay's new mission in life. His students were quite thrilled too. So, what if he did not teach his regular subject. He would be now conducting weekly seminars and counselling sessions. Abhay had also promised that he would also help in clearing doubts in his own subjects whenever he had free time.

"Papa, please come, the food is getting cold. Let us finish dinner soon," Anjali interrupted his trail of thoughts.

The whole week had been busy as well as exciting for Anjali. She had packed all the dresses and other stuff required for their vacation to Malaysia.

It was Vikram and Anjali's 3rd wedding anniversary the next day and it was also their start of trip. Vikram had booked tickets for the afternoon since he wanted to spend at least some time of his anniversary day with Abhay and Anjali's parents, at the same time he wanted the rest of the day to be with Anjali.

As Anjali started setting up the food on the dinner table, Abhay joined them, but he had a big shopping bag with him. Vikram and Anjali looked curiously at the bag while Abhay grinned.

"I have got some gifts for both of you as it is your wedding anniversary tomorrow, actually, I wanted to surprise you two tomorrow but could not contain my excitement and besides, you may have to pack it too. Hope you like it. God bless you both."

Anjali and Vikram quickly opened the bags that he handed over and looked excitedly. It was a beautiful maroon coloured one-piece western wear for Anjali which was perfect for her upcoming holidays. For Vikram, it was a blue denim shorts and a white colour V neck T-shirt having a beach and vacation theme which looked super cool.

"Wow! it is so pretty. I just loved it. How did you manage this, Papa? The colour, style and the fit?" Anjali could not believe her eyes.

Abhay smiled sheepishly. "It is Shivani's selection. Yesterday evening, I had requested her to accompany me to the mall so that I could buy you gifts. I knew that you and Sandhya used to fit in each other's dresses; so, I had taken one of Sandhya's dresses and that is how Shivani could select the right fit; I showed her your photos by which she got some idea about what would suit you and now that you are travelling abroad, it had to be special."

"That was so cool Papa, I really appreciate this and thank you so much; I will call Shivani Ma'am and thank her", Anjali became emotional.

Vikram immediately tried the shorts and the T-shirt, and it was a perfect fit.

Anjali gave a thumbs up. "Vikram, you are going to gain a lot of attention from the females in Malaysia", she teased him while Abhay had a hearty laugh.

Their dinner time went on discussing about their upcoming travel plan with Abhay. Once he mentally noted their plans he said, "Anjali, ask your parents to come home early tomorrow so that we will get to spend the entire morning hours with them. Hope you have told Radhika to reach tomorrow morning by 7am?"

"Yes papa, I have informed Radhika and I'll send a reminder to my parents too", Anjali replied.

Abhay had made a checklist for Anjali and Vikram and asked them to go through it while they do their last moment packing so that they do not miss the essentials.

Anjali's alarm rang at 7 am. She turned to left side and switched off the alarm then turned to her right side to wish Vikram only to find his side of bed to be empty. She thought he would be in the restroom so decided to lie down till he comes out so that she can wish him first thing in the morning.

She waited and waited but when he didn't come out, she called out, "Vicky, where are you?"

"Happy Anniversary!!", she heard 4 distinct voices from right outside her bedroom. She rushed out and was surprised to see her parents, Abhay and Vikram waiting for her with a cake. Vikram gave her a quick hug and wished her.

"Wow! This was a complete surprise! Mom, Dad, you all had secretly planned this and I never got a whiff of this.... wait wait wait...let me quickly freshen up!" saying this she excused herself.

The cake was a yummy red velvet cheesecake and soon all of them relished the cake and clicked some group photos. They all went to Abhay's room where Anjali and Vikram prayed in front of Sandhya's photo.

While Abhay and Anjali's father were chatting, her mother helped Anjali and Vikram with their last-minute packing. Radhika was busy in the kitchen preparing sumptuous lunch for them.

Soon they gathered for a brunch at 11.30am and enjoyed a variety of dishes. For starters, they had corn cutlets, the main course had puri and chole, aloo sabzi, paneer biryani, boondi raita, papad and to add to that Anjali's mother had made yummy carrot halwa for dessert.

Vikram once again made sure the passports, visa and forex were all securely placed in the bags. Their flight to Kuala Lumpur was from Mumbai at 5pm which meant they had to leave their house at 1pm.

As the cab arrived outside the gate, everybody went outside to bid goodbye to Vikram and Anjali.

“Papa are you sure, you will manage yourself, don’t skip your medicines and have lunch and dinner properly. I have instructed Radhika. We will keep you updated from time to time.”, Anjali was saying.

Abhay smiled. “You both have a good time together, explore many new places and don’t worry about anything here.”

Anjali’s mother Sunita hugged her and said, “Don’t worry about Abhay Ji, I and your dad are here for any help he needs and will also meet him from time to time, so you and Vikram beta, just enjoy yourselves.”

She pulled Anjali closer and with a twinkle in her eyes, whispered, “You remember whatever we have discussed right? Happy and safe journey.” Anjali nodded with a sigh.

CHAPTER 18. THE HOLIDAY (PART 1)

"Anju, please hold my laptop bag while I collect our sim cards", Vikram said while he handed over his bag to Anjali. She waited patiently while he activated both their Malaysian sim cards at the Kula Lumpur airport SIM card centre; then made a call to the driver of their pre-booked airport cab. Their hotel in KL was a 45-minute-long drive during which they enjoyed the beautiful night drive accompanied by mild rain showers. It was already late when they had boarded the taxi.

Their driver, Muru, was a tourist friendly person and they could gain a lot of information about Malaysia. He even gave them his views on which places to visit and at what time.

"Sir, how long will you be staying in Malaysia?", Muru asked Vikram.

"Today is 24th right, we are here till 29th August", Vikram replied.

Muru seemed disappointed. "Oh no, sir, 31st August is our Malaysian Independence Day. We celebrate it with great show and enthusiasm. You are going to miss out. There will be lots of decorations and fun everywhere. The whole of Malaysia comes out alive and united."

"Oh, is it? We were not aware of that. We will miss the celebrations." Vikram intoned in disappointment and winked at Anjali. Inwardly, he was relieved; He did not like too much crowd and traffic and any hurdle to his already chalked out plans. They will be out of this place before it happens.

"Why don't you extend your vacation for 2 more days, sir?", Muru suggested.

Vikram was getting a bit irritated now, but managed to smile pleasantly "Hahaha, I wish we could; but getting one week off itself is such a difficult thing you know. I had a tough time convincing my manager to let me go on a break."

"I can understand Sir, life in software companies and all, not very easy. Good that I do not work for any software firm" Muru laughed.

Vikram sighed and went silent and closed his eyes while Anjali was in own her world enjoying the lush green surroundings and the clean sparkling roads; it seemed as if they were moving on a painted canvas.

The lovely lanes, the climate and the 'friendly' driver made them feel as if the 45 minutes just flew by pretty soon. Their hotel was located in the heart of Kuala Lumpur, near the Kuala Lumpur City Centre; they could get a glimpse of the Petronas tower right from their hotel entrance.

"Please call me, Sir; I can take you to different places and I will charge reasonably unlike some others who will simply loot you", Muru suggested and took his fare.

"Sure, we have your number." Vikram smiled and gave a thumbs up. Once Muru had left, Anjali burst out laughing looking at the plastic expressions of Vikram and patted him. They fell in love with the hotel as soon as they entered the grand reception lobby and looked around the plush interiors. The check in procedure took 15 minutes and finally they unlocked their room on the 48th floor. The room itself was breath-taking and the view from the hotel was stunningly beautiful. `

Anjali placed her bag on the nearby table and ran towards the window to capture the view in her heart, as much as possible. They were completely enthralled by what they were viewing from the glass windows. She stood their enjoying the night beauty from her window while Vikram texted his father and her parents and updated them about their new numbers for the next week before joining Anjali near the window.

The clock had struck 1.15 am, it had been a long day and they were tired to hit the hay but the room, the view, and the feeling of having one week only for themselves made them both forget about their tiredness.

"I will go freshen up and change clothes", Anjali said and quickly went to the washroom.

Vikram opened his suitcase using the 3-digit secure pin and kept his night clothes ready.

Soon, they had both freshened up and dressed up in their night clothes and settled down in the bed adjoining the glass windows.

"Vikram, I am suddenly feeling hungry", Anjali complained.

Vikram looked at the time, it was now 2.00 am. "Actually, even I am very hungry."

They had brought a packet of Khakhras; they opened the packets and started hungrily gorging into them. Soon they both finished six of them together.

“I had planned to visit the Batu Caves on the first day that is tomorrow, but I guess we won’t be able to even get up from the bed if we go on like this. We will have to change our plans accordingly”, Vikram was thinking loudly and seriously.

“Chill…this is not your office…we will plan it tomorrow”, saying this, Anjali pulled him close to her and kissed his cheeks and hugged him tightly.

His soft breath on her hair, her hands around his waist, the enchanting room with a view that could turn anyone a lover in their own way, succeeded in playing a magic spell on the young couple and rest of the night witnessed them becoming one passionately.

Their morning dawned with a sense of feeling of one-ness after a long time. They had a lazy morning the next day and got up only at half past ten ending up missing their complimentary breakfast which made Vikram a bit irritated, but Anjali was not too bothered.

They decided to have brunch and leave in the afternoon in order to explore the bird park and the butterfly park for the day before they retire to the room and enjoy the infinity terrace pool on the 52nd floor in their hotel.

Their first place of visit was the Bird Park which was located in the serene and scenic Kuala Lumpur Lake Gardens, a-15-minute drive away from the city centre of Kuala Lumpur. It is a home to more than 3,000 local and foreign birds of approximately 200 different species.

They spent two hours enjoying the view of the flying beauties and learnt about the free-flight concept followed in this park which allow the birds to breed naturally in this unique environment. They left to their next destination after the mandatory photos with the birds.

The butterfly park was close to the bird park, so they decided to walk the distance enjoying the natural beauty. The butterfly park is the largest butterfly garden in the world which shelters over 5000 live butterflies, exotic plants, butterfly-host plants, and ferns.

“The Japanese koi fish, freshwater turtles, live insects and a museum with a large collection of butterflies and insects from around the world are not to be missed when you visit the butterfly park in Malaysia”, Diya had told Vikram.

They decided to visit KL City Centre to grab some Indian dinner before returning to their room.

“Hello papa! how are you? We are having our dinner now”, Vikram spoke to Abhay.

“Hi Beta, I’m fine. How was your day? Is Anjali enjoying the stay?”, Abhay enquired. Their talk lasted for 2 minutes quickly updating each other about their day.

“Papa, I’ll video call you using the Wi-Fi tomorrow morning from our room and show you the beauty. We are going to Batu Caves tomorrow morning. Take care”, said Vikram.

They were too tired when they entered the hotel; they decided to skip the infinity pool for that day and sleep so that the next morning, they could visit the mesmerizing Batu Caves.

CHAPTER 19. THE HOLIDAY (PART 2)

"Wow!! The view from the room is surreal! And the room itself is so aesthetically designed and awesome amenities", exclaimed Abhay.

"Papa, ask Anjali's parents to have a look too…", Vikram said. Sunita and Rajesh had invited Abhay for the breakfast and all five got busy over the video call.

"Hi Anju! Done with breakfast? Hope you are not facing issue with regards to the food", Sunita asked the typical mommy question once she saw her daughter. "Yes, Mom, just finished breakfast; no problem at all. The food is amazing here. We will be proceeding to Batu caves in a while", Anjali said as she waved at her dad and Abhay.

"Good, Enjoy and keep sharing pics!", Rajesh spoke and wound up the call so that their kids proceed as per the plan without getting delayed.

They felt fresher than the previous day and were all set to start their journey to Batu caves and Kuala Gandah Elephant Sanctuary.

"I had read about Batu caves during school days and recently came across the details while I helped our neighbour for her project on Batu caves. Do you know the limestone forming Batu Caves is said to be around 400 million years old?", asked Anjali as they neared their destination; Vikram was astonished to hear that.

The travel from their hotel to Batu caves took about 45 minutes. The wide lanes, pleasant weather, the tall structures in one stretch and greeneries in the next stretch served as a treat to their eyes and mind.

"Wow!! What an architectural marvel!", exclaimed Vikram as he moved forward holding Anjali's hands. Both of them were unable to take their eyes off the world's tallest statue of Lord Murugan (also known as Karthikeya), a Hindu deity, standing 140 ft high, located outside the Batu Caves. The serenity and the exhilaration that filled in their hearts was beyond explanation.

They slowly read the History about the statue and Anjali pointed at one of the lines which read –

The statue, which cost approximately 24 million rupees, is made of 1550 cubic metres of concrete, 250 tonnes of steel bars and 300 litres of gold paint brought in from neighbouring Thailand.

The Batu Caves temple complex consists of three main caves and a few smaller ones. The biggest, referred to as Cathedral Cave or Temple Cave, has a 100 m-high ceiling and features ornate Hindu shrines. To reach it, visitors must climb a steep flight of 272 steps.

Vikram and Anjali enjoyed climbing the flight of stairways and after climbing up every 25 to 30 steps turned to admire the statue and looked at front to appreciating the beauty of the cave entrance, so that they can catch their breath and get ready for the next few steps.

As they entered the cave, the mesmerising architecture and the beautiful idols took Anjali and Vikram almost 2 hours to completely know the history of the place and enjoy the positive vibrations sitting in the cave. They clicked as many photos as they could.

Vikram sat at a place and silently watched the limestone formations and they seemed to symbolise different shapes and objects. As he silently prayed and meditated, he felt Sandhya's presence around him. He felt he was very close to his mother, and it seemed like she was waving and smiling back at him.

When they left from there, they silently replayed the beauty they witnessed in their mind, when they travelled towards Kuala Gandah, the elephant sanctuary. This travel was full of greeneries on both sides of the road.

There was an elephant awareness show going on when they reached the place, and the host was explaining how elephants are being poached for ivory and the various other items. He also was giving instructions on how to interact with the animals, for feeding or bathing them.

Vikram purchased two packets of small pieces of sugar cane sticks each consisting of five pieces, and they picked up spots to feed the elephants. Anjali was a bit apprehensive initially but once the elephant took the first piece from her, she was all for it and excitedly started feeding the rest while Vikram was taking her candid pictures. All the visitors then gathered at a spot from which they gazed at the lake below where six elephants were being bathed by the staff. From the look and expressions of the elephants, it was evident that they were having a gala time and they were playing with each other and splashing water. It was so much fun to see this, and all the small kids were clapping and laughing.

They spent an hour more in the sanctuary before boarding the cab for the return journey. Anjali rested her head on Vikram's shoulder while Vikram scrolled through the pics that they had clicked. "Wow…this one is a perfect click", Anjali told as the screen displayed a pic in which she was feeding the elephant some sugarcane pieces and both Anjali and the elephant looked in the direction of the camera making it seem as if both were posing exclusively for the camera.

"We have reached your hotel, sir", the driver called and that's when Anjali and Vikram woke up from their power nap. "Let us go to the room and continue our sleep for some more time", Anjali said while trying to control her yawn. It was around 4 pm.

"Let us go to the pool in the evening. Till then you rest", Vikram said as their lift reached the 48th floor. They had an amazing pool time later that evening. The infinity pool was one of its kind and from the pool the entire KL city appeared before them in its full grandeur.

Later they had their dinner and went for a walk in the moonlit night. Anjali held Vikram's hands tightly and whispered, "This is the best vacation for me, and it is not over yet; Thank you so much Vicky for making this anniversary so special for me."

Vikram too held her hands and said solemnly, "I am sorry I have not been giving you time since the last one year, we were all lost in our own grief, and you never complained once, you have always supported me and Papa and took care of us, Anju."

The next day, the third and final day in Kula Lumpur was spent in shopping, visiting the Aquaria KLCC which is an amazing showcase of 5000 land and aquatic creatures and the Petronas Towers.

The KL stay came to an end with their plans being nicely executed, thus gearing them up for their next destination in Malaysia, the Langkawi Islands.

They were eagerly looking forward to do the Island Hopping, enjoy the Sky Bridge and the Langkawi cable car rides and take photos in the magical 3D Art Museum.

They checked out from their hotel in KL and proceeded to the airport and Anjali silently gazed around from her cab reminiscing all the moments that they had shared in the last 3 days.

CHAPTER 20. THE GOSSIP

“Any updates from Vikram and Anjali? Hope they are having a gala time” asked Shivani as she entered Abhay’s cabin. She had brought Methi Puris and Aloo Jeera sabzi for lunch. It was almost 2pm now.

Abhay was so engrossed in paperwork for the upcoming seminar that he was completely oblivious to her presence and looked up only after hearing her question. “Hey sorry, didn’t see you entering. I am almost done with the preparation for the seminar. Yes, spoke to Vikram in the morning. He said today they will be checking out from KL and proceeding to Langkawi Islands”, smiled Abhay.

“Wow. That’s really nice. Langkawi is a beautiful island. I had been there a long time ago. It is completely serene, and you will feel like never coming out of it”, Shivani spoke as she occupied the chair opposite to him and opened her lunch box and suggested, “You should take a solo trip Abhay. It is so much fun to explore places. You will learn a lot and it gives an experience which you can never put in words for others to understand but it will leave you with a lot of satisfaction and boost up your confidence not to mention that it will improve your general knowledge”, she laughed.

“I agree with you, but I’ll start missing Sandhya as I have never visited any new place alone after marriage…though she had travelled alone for her official trips, they were never more than a week, I am not too confident about it”, Abhay responded as he opened his lunch box.

Shivani nodded. Still there was more work to do with Abhay, she mentally noted. She had to boost his confidence and create an opportunity for him to travel alone and gain confidence.

She served him two puris and the sabzi. Abhay opened his lunch box and took in the fragrance.

"Shivani, you should try this; Radhika has made gatte ki sabzi and chapatis. God bless that child…you should meet her once. What a hard-working girl she is!" Abhay appraised Radhika as he served one chapati and gate ki sabzi to Shivani.

"Yes, Abhay, it is a long pending visit; will surely visit your place with Ajay once Vikram and Anjali are back."

Their lunch time discussion travelled from discussing her experiences during various countries' visits and the experiences and learnings she had; to their current project on discussing ideas to execute their next steps effectively.

Post lunch, Abhay opened his laptop and showed her the presentation he had prepared for his session in his college. She suggested a few minor corrections and he quickly revised the points that he will be covering in the session.

This session will serve as an introduction to the next day's program which will guide the students on the smart selection of the career from the available options followed by Shivani's session on how to stay away from office politics and keep improving our skills to find a stable place in the work field.

The introductory session started sharp at 4pm and for the next one hour, Abhay gave the third year and final year engineering students a clear picture about the next day's session so that they can come prepared with their queries and their requirements.

Abhay and Shivani wound up their session at 5pm and stepped out of the college auditorium accompanied by Ajay.

"Sir, the moment we came to know you will be associated with our college and taking seminars, we were thrilled... A few of us have got some doubts in our final year projects. If possible, can you please clarify our doubts whenever you are free?" Ajay asked Abhay.

Abhay patted Ajay on his back and said, "Sure, my boy, next week I'll come to the college again. I will keep you and the HOD in the loop and decide the day."

Ajay was elated to hear this and thanked him. He moved back to the auditorium after Shivani's car exited the college campus back to their studio.

"I have a splitting headache. Can we stop for tea break?" Abhay asked as Shivani proceeded to drop him home.

"Sure, but why suddenly; are you tensed about the seminar? Are you taking your medicines properly?" Shivani got worried as she looked out for a parking near Hanuman hotel.

As they stepped out of the car, she could sense that Abhay was not well and may even need a medical intervention. He was unable to walk towards the hotel and that's when Shivani decided to take him to the hospital.

The doctor monitored his pulse and confirmed a sudden shoot in his blood pressure and gave him an injection. He informed

Shivani that some rest, no caffeine, proper food with less salt and exercise will keep him fine. He was kept under observation for 2 hours before Shivani finished the payment and discharge procedures. "Abhay, nothing to worry; come I'll drop you home", Shivani said.

Once they settled in the car, Abhay said, "thank you so much Shivani, did Vikram or Anjali call? Where is my phone? They will be worried if I miss their calls."

"Abhay, they had texted you and shared few photos; but I have not opened the chats; the notification kept popping. You call them now while I drive you back home", Shivani said and started the car after handing over Abhay's mobile.

Abhay called them but did not get any response. "Guess my kids are busy", he told Shivani with a smile and checked his watch to calculate the Malaysian time. "It should be 10pm there; must have slept early. Let me check the messages", Abhay told Shivani while he opened his WhatsApp messenger and checked the photos; Vikram and Anjali had shared photos of the hotel where they were staying. There were few messages about the place and one message from Anjali saying, "Papa, we will be going for a walk after dinner and explore the hotel; Will not be taking our mobiles as we have kept it for charging…call you once we get back to our room".

"Shivani, do you think I should say about this? I feel I should not bother them with these details now. Let them enjoy their vacation, right?" asked Abhay referring to the hospital visit.

"Abhay, I feel you should inform them. These two are the ones who genuinely care for you. Do inform them but tell them in a subtle way so that they do not get worried", Shivani told as she parked her car and added "Abhay, we have reached your building; I'm planning to visit your home today and have dinner with you; if that is fine with you", she added. Abhay knew that this sudden decision was taken by her to keep a check on his health, food, and medicines; he smiled and nodded in affirmative.

As they entered the lift lobby, they met Mr and Mrs. Shukla who stayed one floor above them. Abhay introduced Shivani to them, and they exchanged pleasantries. They soon excused themselves and got out of the lift on the third floor. Abhay rummaged his bag to get the house keys and Shivani helped him unlock the house. She looked around as soon as Abhay sat on the sofa and had some water. She looked around the house and studied the artistic paintings on the wall.

"These were made by Sandhya in her college times. She was such an artist. I insisted on framing them and using for home décor." Abhay's voice was full of appreciation for Sandhya and the tiredness that he had a few moments earlier had somehow vanished.

Meanwhile, Mrs. Shukla was busy in a discussion with her husband. She was the typical 'gossip aunty' whom any sensible person in their life would steer clear of. Mr. Shukla did not like her habit and often reprimanded her for talking ill of people behind their back. Mrs. Shukla continued, "I wonder who that lady is with Mr. Singh. He says she is his colleague. Wonder why he brought her home, at this hour! That too when his son and daughter-in-law are abroad. You never know, anything can happen nowadays!", she said with an exasperated sigh.

CHAPTER 21. THE ODYSSEY

Two months had passed since Vikram and Anjali had returned from their Malaysia trip. They all were busy moving forward in their lives, especially, Abhay who got involved in his new job completely and his health condition too improved to a great deal. Vikram was busy learning a new technology as part of his current assignment, and it required him to spend more time in office, but he did not complain as it was more out of his passion rather than anyone pressurising him. Anjali too found more time to pursue her hobbies as she was now much more relieved about Abhay and Vikram. Things were going normal although they all missed Sandhya in some way or the other.

"Papa, please check if you have packed the essentials or not", Anjali said as she started jotting down the essentials. It was a Saturday and Vikram was busy helping his dad with the packing. "This is the first time I'm going on an official tour", murmured Abhay, "My previous job never required any outstation visits."

'Don't worry Papa, you will get a good experience. What is your schedule for the next 3 days?', enquired Vikram as he neatly placed a towel on the top and closed the trolley.

Abhay and Shivani were invited by a college in Goa for a 3-day counselling seminar with the students. Shivani found this to be an ideal opportunity for Abhay to explore the world and come out of his inhibitions. It needed some coaxing from everyone, but finally Abhay accepted it. The college authorities had booked 2-tier AC train tickets for them from Mumbai to Goa.

“Tomorrow morning, we will reach Goa and check in at the hotel they have booked…some resort…I forgot the name…wait I’ll check and tell”, Abhay thought hard trying to remember the name as he opened the voucher, “D-Ville beach resort. Remembering such complicated names were always Sandhya’s cup of tea so I never bothered to learn the pronunciations”, chuckled Abhay and started summarising his trip details, “We have sessions and workshops on Monday, Tuesday, and Wednesday. It will be from 10.30am to 12.30pm and then again from 1.30pm till 3.30pm every day, after that we are free for the rest of the day. We will checkout post dinner on Wednesday and reach Mumbai on Thursday morning”, Abhay concluded.

Vikram and Anjali dropped Abhay at the railway station at 9pm, an hour before the train departure, where Shivani was waiting for them at the entrance. They all were so busy discussing about the places that they can explore in Goa on the next day as well as during the weekdays in the evening that they did not realise that time passed too soon, and their train arrived. “Papa, please take your medicines on time and rest well. Have a good time both of you”, Vikram said as they waved them goodbye.

It was a pleasant Sunday morning when Abhay and Shivani reached Goa and proceeded towards the exit where a pleasant looking cab driver, arranged by the college authorities, was waiting for them.

"Hello, Sir, Madam, my name is Martin D' Mello, very nice to meet you and welcome to Goa", he smiled, shaking their hands. They were travelling through the picturesque lanes of Goa and the fresh air, and the traffic free road were captivating them.

"Martin, we want to visit a couple of places today evening. Would it be possible for you?" Shivani asked him. He nodded as they listed out the places and asked how much time it would take to cover and how much they owed him.
Their resort was quite expansive and lots of guests were seen busy moving around. There were many foreigners too. The reception lobby was grand, and they were served welcome drinks as they completed their check-in formalities. They got 2 adjacent deluxe rooms on the 3rd floor with a poolside view from their balconies. They got ready and met down for an early lunch in the restaurant where they enjoyed the Goan delicacies.
Abhay decided he wanted to take a nap for a while and said he would meet Shivani at 3.30pm and she instructed Martin accordingly.

Abhay and Shivani got into the cab at 3:30pm where Martin was waiting for them. Soon they reached the first spot, as per the plan, the famous 'Our Lady of Health' church.

As Abhay looked around, he felt an overwhelming peace from within. He slowly walked towards the entrance thinking all the happy moments he had spent with Sandhya. As he prayed, he became emotional, and tears started filling in his eyes. Shivani did not say anything and did not intrude his personal space. He sat on the bench and closed his eyes and felt Sandhya's presence near him. Finally, he held himself up and joined Shivani who was exploring the architectural beauty of the Church.

"Are you fine Abhay? Do you need some time more?", Shivani asked with a smile. "No. I am fine Shivani. Thanks for being so understanding. You know, I never thought I will be able to go out anywhere without Sandhya. But here I am, of course, I miss her, but I feel stronger now and I know I am not alone, there are people who love and care for me; all thanks to you", replied to a contended Abhay.

"I am proud of you Abhay. This is how I wanted you to be. The Universe will always guide us when we need help or when we are in trouble; all we need to do is recognise the help it is offering and work hard to utilise the opportunity", she patted him.

The second destination that Martin took them to was the Velsao Beach. He was full of praise for the beach. "This beach has sugar sand and is so serene and beautiful. One can visit the Three Kings church on top of the mountain which overlooks the entire village of Velsao Cansaulim and the Arabian sea. This is a secluded beach where not many tourists visit. It's pristine clean and the traditional fishing still goes on. Great venue for photography. In December, the sea gulls come in hundreds; you get really nice seashells for collection. Just walk around the beach for a while and enjoy the sunset".

Abhay and Shivani walked around for an hour in the sugar sand pristine beach and were mesmerised by the beauty of the sunset. They could find very few tourists and some local fisherman here and there. Finally, they left the beach and got back to their rooms exhausted.

The next 3 days were quite exhilarating as well as enjoyable for Abhay and Shivani. She too found this to be a new experience as till now she had been doing this alone but now having Abhay with her gave her a more fruitful and a learning experience as well as a good company.

It was finally time to bid adieu to Goa and get back home. Shivani's car driver had come to pick them up in Mumbai and first she dropped Abhay home where Anjali was eagerly waiting for them.
She had already invited Shivani for lunch and though Shivani had declined politely initially but after Anjali's multiple persuasions, she had agreed.

As they proceeded towards the lift area, Mrs Shukla was excitedly chatting with her friends said, "it seems Anjali has found a new mother-in-law…do you know…the other day that lady colleague of Mr. Singh visited his home when the children were abroad; now I hear that they both went on some business trip together. I had also seen her visit the Singh's home on two other occasions…something must be brewing for sure".

Though Shivani and Abhay did not hear this, it didn't escape the ears of the fuming Anjali who felt like delivering a punch on Mrs. Shukla's face right then and there.

CHAPTER 22. THE CELEBRATION

Abhay got up early that morning. It was a beautiful morning with pleasant sun rays falling on him through the windows. He yawned and looked at the clock. It was 6.00 am. He looked at Sandhya's photo and smiled. She smiled back at him through the frame, and he felt her utter those words, "Wish you a very happy birthday, my dearest hubby", Sandhya would always wish him that way on his birthday.

"Wish you a very happy birthday Papa!!", Vikram and Anjali tore into his room chorusing.

Abhay blinked at them surprised. Usually, they got up by 7.30 am. Vikram gave a warm hug and wished again. "Thanks very much, my dear children", he smiled. They all gazed at Sandhya's photo for a while.

"Papa, I have made your favourite Sevaiya Kheer in the same way as Mummyji used to prepare on each birthday; now, get ready and have a bowl of it." Anjali said. Vikram handed over a bag to Abhay and said, "Papa, hope you like it." Abhay found that it was a very nice blue cotton kurta from Fab India. It was quite stylish and appealing.

"Sorry, Papa, I will have to go to office today as we have a major Go-Live of our application", Vikram apologised.

"Na, it is completely fine. I also will have to go to the Studio today and complete a pile of pending tasks.", Abhay rued.

"Well, well, you both forgot about me, I will also leave for Second Innings then", Anjali groaned.

Vikram gave her a thumbs up once Abhay went for bath. They had planned a surprise party for Abhay in the evening and had invited Anjali's parents, Ajay, and Shivani too. Vikram planned to leave half day from office and directly come to 'Hang Out', the restaurant where they had arranged to celebrate the birthday party.

"I have spoken to Ravi Mama and Reema Mami. They said everything is sorted", Vikram told her. Ravi, who was Vikram's maternal uncle and Sandhya's younger brother, had returned from London, a couple of weeks ago. He, along with his wife, had gone there to extend their helping hand to their daughter who had delivered their grandson a few months before.

Shivani and other members in the "Just Be There" studio celebrated Abhay's birthday by cutting cake and ordering pizza and cold drinks as per the demand by the youngsters of the group. "Thank you very much, my dear friends. I really had a wonderful birthday celebration with all of you", Abhay was emotional.

Post Lunch, Abhay was immersed in his work for the next couple of hours until Shivani knocked his cabin door. "Abhay, let us visit the Ganesh Temple at half past five near the Star Mall today." Abhay agreed. Shivani had been entrusted with the job of getting Abhay to the restaurant by 6pm which was inside the Star Mall.

Shivani and Abhay had an amazing darshan at the Ganesh temple and they both sat at the temple premises for some time enjoying the silence and the serenity.

Shivani got a call on her mobile and excused herself. She soon returned and said, "Abhay, I just got a call from a friend, I had ordered a pack of home décor items. She is inside Star Mall now and it is just a 2-minute walk from here as you know, can we quickly go and collect it? I promise it will not take more than 10 minutes", Shivani's eyes were pleading and so Abhay could not refuse.

They reached the 2nd level of the mall where the restaurant was located, and Shivani led him through the entrance. Abhay was completely stunned and struggled for words as he saw Vikram, Anjali, Ravi and Reema waving at him and cheering. He felt a tap on his shoulder and turned to face Ajay who was grinning "Happy birthday, dear Sir", he shook hands with Abhay and winked at the others.

Abhay gave Shivani a surprised and a mock angry look and received a wink and a chuckle from her; their friendly equation didn't go unnoticed by the others present there. As they all gathered for a cake cutting, Vikram and Anjali requested the hotel staff to bring the birthday cake out in the middle.

As Abhay opened the cake box, the cute pair of tiny shoes carved with cream in the centre of the chocolate cake caught everyone's eyes and almost instantly, all pairs of eyes widened and gazed at a blushing Anjali and smiling Vikram. Abhay stood rooted to the spot with all kinds of emotions running through his mind.

"Papa, please go ahead and read the card next to the cake, aloud", Vikram prompted Abhay.

Abhay reached for the greeting card and with trembling hands, read the note inside aloud as everyone stood transfixed.

“Hello, Daadu, a very happy birthday to you, yes you guessed it right, I am on my way to meet you all very soon. Daadi has already told me to give you lots of love and make sure you are always happy and kept busy. Once I come out from Mamma’s tummy, I am going to make you run and dance and sing and play every day with me. So better prepare yourself. Love you a lot ??”

Abhay’s eyes were filled with tears of joy and hugged Vikram and Anjali.

“This is the best birthday gift I could have received, thank you so much and God bless the three of you. Sandhya would have jumped in joy if she was here”, he blessed the would-be parents.

Sunita’s eyes welled up with happy tears as she hugged Anjali and kissed her; Abhay and Rajesh congratulated each other and wrapped Vikram in their arms and blessed him.

Vikram and Anjali took blessings from his mama and mami and proceeded towards Shivani who heartily congratulated both and said, “You will be an exemplary set of parents. All will be fine.” Her words boosted their confidence.

“Wow, I’ll be chachu soon…lovely, isn’t it? I will shift my base to your home and play with the little one during my vacation”, Ajay exclaimed looking at Vikram. Vikram gave him a brotherly side hug and said, “Yes, my bro! you are always welcome.”

The evening was accompanied with laughter, chit-chats about the old times, some present college and office life and Sandhya. The double celebration ended by 9pm and as everyone took leave, they asked Anjali to take care of her health and offered to help, if and whenever needed.

"I am really happy to see Abhay Jiju coming back to normal after having gone through so much trauma and suffering after Sandhya Didi's demise", Ravi was telling Reema as they were going home in their cab.

"Yes, Ravi, after he was in the state that we saw him last time, I never thought he would bounce back in life. He had completely gone into a shell. Anjali said that he has improved a lot ever since he joined Shivani's Yoga studio. It was Shivani who counselled Abhay Jiju into living his life again." Reema told him.

"Actually, they do share a good chemistry. She seems to be a very understanding and a sensible person; Jiju needs company too in his life....", as Ravi was finding the right words, Reema understood his intentions and completed his thoughts by saying, "I too actually thought about it, but let us keep this to ourselves, for now", Reema agreed.

Meanwhile at Abhay's place as everyone retired to their rooms, Vikram and Anjali replayed the photos and videos multiple times, which was shared by Ajay of the birthday celebrations, especially Abhay's elation when he had read the note which they had beautifully penned for him.

CHAPTER 23. THE PROPOSITION

Anjali was enjoying the completion of her first trimester. The last few weeks had been quite exhilarating for her. She experienced a new side of herself where she was swinging into a plethora of moods, sometimes too happy, sometimes too frustrated, and sometimes feeling too low. Abhay and Vikram knew that the new feeling of motherhood was making Anjali moody, and they did their best to support her and keep her cheerful and motivated. Her mother would visit every day and bring her different diet food as prescribed by her gynaecologist.

It was a Saturday morning and Anjali and Vikram were coming back after their monthly sonography appointment. Abhay had gone out to attend the wedding of one of his group mates of 'Just Be There' Studio. They met Mrs and Mr. Shukla at the parking lot where the couple was taking out two big bags from their car.

"How are you doing Anjali beta? Doctor's appointment, is it?", Mr. Shukla asked with a genuine smile as he noticed them carrying their sonography files.

"Yes Uncle, going on fine, enjoying the new phase", smiled Anjali as Mrs Shukla joined them in the conversation.

"We saw your father-in-law in the morning as he was going out with that lady friend of his, what's her name…I keep forgetting…Shivani, right? I even waved at them, but they did not notice; they seemed to be in a hurry", she added with a smirk.

"Yes, Aunty, they must be definitely in a hurry as she had to pick up two more people as they are attending one of their yoga mate's wedding today." Anjali replied promptly with a slight irritation in her voice. Mr. Shukla and Vikram both looked at each other and took their ladies away excusing themselves.

"I really pity Shukla uncle, he is such a genuine person and a gentleman, but his wife is a complete opposite", Anjali told Vikram as they stepped inside their house.

"As they say, opposites attract", laughed Vikram. "Just like how I am a gentleman, and you are…", he started when Anjali pinched him. "You are what? What did you say now?", Anjali glowered at him. "Hey, cool, I was just kidding, now stop jumping around and sit carefully", Vikram said as he helped her on the sofa.

"Some people are just incorrigible; ignore them. One of my office colleagues too spotted Papa with Ms. Shivani once and the way he told me, I found it weird as his tone was filled more with curiosity to know if there was something more than friendship between the two.", Vikram said.

"You know what Vikram, I have been thinking about this for some time now, but I was not sure how to tell you this; since the topic has started, let me tell. Do you think that there can be a future for Papa and Shivani Aunty together in case they wish to be with each other? What will be your take on it? Will you be able to accept her?" Anjali asked him solemnly.

Vikram's face was anguished but he smiled, "I know it is very hard for me to say this. I know people will talk either way and be judgemental about whatever we do. I may never be able to accept Ms. Shivani as my mother or stepmother, but, if Papa does have any feelings and he wishes to marry her, then I will not be a hurdle to their relationship. I will accept her as a family member. The choice is theirs, but we can let him know that we are open to this idea. I mean he should not think that we will not accept and for our sake, lead a different life, right? I know how much she has done for Papa and us too, and I am always grateful to her for that", his eyes were moist as Anjali hugged him.

It was almost 9.30pm when Abhay reached home. Vikram and Anjali had finished their dinner and were watching TV. Abhay freshened up and reclined on the sofa. He started narrating the events that transpired that day and how they had enjoyed the whole wedding and reception party. Abhay was in a very jovial and pleasant mood, so Vikram and Anjali decided this was the best time to let him know what they felt.

"We are so happy, Papa, it seems like you had a gala time at the wedding. You, joining the studio with Shivani aunty was one of the best decisions you took." Vikram said unsure of how to continue.

"Yes, beta, wherever Shivani is, the mood automatically becomes light. She has that kind of an aura to make any one happy and cheerful" Abhay agreed.

"We have seen that you both share a great camaraderie and understand each other really well. She has been your pillar of strength and determination from the moment she has stepped into your life. Papa, if at all, in the future, you both feel that you can be each other's life partners and wish to be together, we are always with you and will always support your decisions and we want to tell you that even mom would wish that you remain happy."

Abhay was completely shocked by what he had heard from Vikram and Anjali and his eyes welled with emotions.

"Vikram and Anjali, what is wrong with you, children? How could you even think that I have any such plans and that I could possibly think of a future with Shivani? I don't care about the society, and I don't know what made you both think on those lines. if it is because of those neighbours' gossip talks, let me tell you this very clearly now that Sandhya was, is and will always be my wife, my life partner and in fact, my soul mate. I can never accept or even think of someone else as my wife. Sandhya's memories are so completely filled in my heart that there is no place for someone else. I can spend my entire lifetime reminiscing those moments and the emotions that we both shared. I live with Sandhya every day and she is never amiss from my life.

My life is now dedicated for helping others and making this society a better place. And I am trying my best to contribute my bit to the society, and this has been possible with the help of Shivani; I owe her a lot for this. Shivani is my mentor, my guide, a confidante, and my colleague. Often, we face problems that we feel cannot be addressed to our family and in such cases, we rather confide in our close friends whom we know will find a solution or be a soothing balm to heal it instead of adding extra woes to the problem. Shivani is that kind of friend to me. Don't you have such friends Vikram and Anjali? I am sure you do and confide in them what you may or may not be able to tell me or to each other. And that is absolutely fine. That doesn't mean that you will be looking for a love relationship with them, right?".

Vikram and Anjali too had tears in their eyes as Abhay had now stopped speaking and his face was bereft of any emotions. He was completely calm and composed and was looking at them solemnly.

"We are so proud of you Papa", Anjali finally found her voice as Vikram gave Abhay a tight hug. "We are very sorry if we offended you in any way, but we just thought that you should never feel left out and that we will always support you", she said.

"I am not at all angry with you. And I am happy that you came out in the open rather than keeping within you and assuming things that you should not be doing. I am also proud that my children are very practical and openminded. With both of you on my side, do you think that I will ever be alone? I know that the past one year had left us all on a brink and we really could not properly support one another, but now we have all pulled ourselves up with Shivani's help. To add to it, our junior will arrive shortly. So, my entire day is going to be busy playing with my grandchild. Remember, I have to be both Daadu and Daadi for the kid? My family is all I want and nothing else. And I and Shivani will always be there for each other as the thickest of friends but not as life partners", Abhay said no more and retired to his room. Vikram and Anjali took in all that they heard and silently retired to their rooms.

They all were, in a way, relieved and knew that the topic would not bother them anymore even if others in the society talked about it. After all, it is the acceptance that comes from the family which matters, rather than the societal prejudices.

(EPILOGUE)
CHAPTER 24. THE ARRIVAL

Six months later.

Abhay was working on his laptop at the studio in the afternoon, post lunch, when his mobile rang. It was from Rajesh, Anjali's father.

"Abhay Ji, please hurry up, Anju has developed labour pains, we are taking her to the hospital, you also come there directly. I have informed Vikram, he is on his way and will reach in another 45 mins.", Rajesh informed.

"Sure, Rajesh ji, I am leaving immediately", Abhay replied and started to pack his bag. He went to Shivani and told her about the development. Shivani too got ready and said that she will accompany him to the hospital.

They soon reached the hospital and met Rajesh and Sunita who were pacing nervously in the labour ward.

"What did the doctor say, is Anjali alright?", Abhay asked with concern.

"Yes, they have taken her inside, it seems the baby's head is facing up. They are going to wait for twenty more minutes, otherwise they may have to do a forceps", Sunita's voice was shaky and almost crying.

"Don't worry, Sunita Ji, all will be fine, the baby will be delivered soon, let us all pray for a smooth delivery", Shivani comforted her as Vikram came up to them running and panting.

They filled him in with the latest updates and he nodded nervously. Everyone became silent for the next 15mins, and they all prayed inwardly for a smooth delivery and for the baby and mom's safety.

Finally, they heard a small cry from inside the labour room and looked up eagerly.

The doctor came out after some time holding the baby in a pink hued cloth wrap and called Vikram.

"Congratulations, Sir, you have become father to a lovely baby girl", she said with a big smile and Vikram slowly took the baby in his arms with full of happiness as well as nervousness. The tenseness disappeared the moment his baby girl flashed a toothless smile at him; he held her close to his heart and planted a peck full of assurances, on her forehead.

"Your wife will regain consciousness after an hour, she is perfectly fine, your baby is very stubborn; she had changed her position and gave us a tough time to get her out, she is a cute naughty little angel", the doctor gently caressed the baby and Vikram smiled proudly.

The others soon joined Vikram and took turns to hold the baby and caress her. Finally, it was Abhay's turn, and he slowly and gently took her in his arms and gazed lovingly at the small baby. The baby seemed to give a faint smile at him.

"She has got Sandhya's features, Vikram, see the smile, and the eyes, don't you think?", Abhay said to Vikram as Vikram nodded.

"Yes Papa, I sincerely believe that mom has returned back to us as my daughter", as he patted Abhay's shoulders.

When the others were busy playing and caressing the baby, Shivani had quickly sneaked out to call Ajay and get sweet boxes for the doctors and hospital staff. She along with Ajay soon returned with 3 to 4 big boxes of sweets and asked Abhay to distribute the same to everyone. Abhay thanked her for her sweet gesture. Soon Anjali had regained her consciousness and took her baby in her arms with smiles and tears and all sorts of emotions running within herself.

"What name have you thought for the baby, Bhaiya and Bhabhi?", Ajay asked them. The baby was now sleeping serenely on her small crib next to Anjali's bed.

"It is going to be a special name, Ajay", Vikram said looking at Anjali and she smiled.

"We are naming her as Sabhya, after Sandhya ma and Abhay papa", Anjali revealed.

Abhay became emotional hearing this and wiped the drop of tears flowing clearly now.

"Wow, that's really a special name Vikram", Shivani congratulated him and Abhay once again and added, "Sabhya also means well mannered, and I am pretty sure she will live up to her name".

Abhay crept out of the room and sat on a chair outside and closed his eyes. "Thank you so much Sandhya for coming back in our lives as Vikram's daughter. Please continue to just be there."

****** The Beginning ******

AUTHOR'S NOTE

Dear Readers,

Hope you enjoyed the journey of Abhay, Shivani, Vikram, and Anjali. Thank you for reading and I am grateful to you all. I request your valuable and honest feedback which will keep me further motivated.

I would love to emphasise on two of the crucial words of one's life, acceptance, and support. When a child enters the world, as its family, embrace the child, accept its gender, its calibre, stop comparison and support its choices. The child comes to the world and is connected only to its family before knowing its friends and society. As a family, your acceptance and support are what matter to the child more than the societal acknowledgement.

Many a times, we are tempted to be judgemental about others from our standpoint of view. If one stops being judgemental, automatically acceptance and support will follow. When an individual is blessed with an understanding family, he or she will garner understanding friends who become his or her extended family and the society has no other choice but to accept and support the individual who has sufficient backing from his family and friends.

#JustBeThere for your family and your friends by just accepting and supporting them when they face a crisis. The world would then be a much better place to live in. Stay Blessed!

Yours Sincerely,

Gayatri Shankar